She had a feeling Nat would be there

She had been told the restaurant was the haunt of foreign journalists and Marianne waited and watched the entrance. And then, when waiting had cooled her mood of elation, the door swung open and she saw Nat standing there, eyes narrowed against the sudden bright lights. About to call his name, she realized he was not alone. And with a chill sense of dismay she recognized the red gold hair and slanting green eyes of Lisette.

So numbing was the shock that she could only stare. Then, when she realized that they had passed—Nat not even noticing her—it seemed she actually heard her world crumbling.

All she wanted was to get away—to get away.

MARY BURCHELL

is also the author
of the following titles in

HARLEQUIN CLASSIC LIBRARY

Paris - and My Love

MARY BURCHELL

Originally published as Harlequin Romance #565

HARLEQUIN
CLASSIC LIBRARY

TORONTO • LONDON • LOS ANGELES • AMSTERDAM
SYDNEY • HAMBURG • PARIS • STOCKHOLM • ATHENS • TOKYO

Original hardcover edition published by
Mills & Boon Limited 1960
ISBN 0-373-80013-4

Harlequin edition first published January 1961
Golden Harlequin Library edition, Volume XXXVII,
published September 1973
Harlequin Classic Library edition published April 1980

Second printing March 1981

CHAPTER ONE

"BUT, MADAME—" resolutely, Marianne faced the director of the great fashion house of Florian "—if you will not give me a chance to show what I can do, how do you know I am not suited for the job?"

"It is not necessary to eat an egg in order to know that it is bad," replied Madame Moisant with her customary candor.

Marianne blanched slightly at the unflattering simile. But she wanted this job too badly to surrender without a struggle. Besides, there was a streak of obstinacy in her that refused to allow her to accept defeat on what she judged to be unfair grounds.

"I've never been compared to a bad egg before," she confessed with a rueful smile, "but—"

"The comparison was purely figurative, *mademoiselle*."

"But won't you at least tell me why you're so sure that Monsieur Florian wouldn't even consider me as a model?" Marianne pressed. "Without being conceited, I know I have most of the qualifications needed for displaying clothes well. And as you see, I have really excellent references from the firm for whom I worked in London. Not an inconsiderable firm, either, *madame*."

"One of the leading stores," agreed Madame Moisant, with a passing glance at the letters Marianne had placed before her. "Possibly even *the* leading store," she admitted a trifle grudgingly. "But I presume that there you displayed dresses that had already been designed and made before you ever came into the picture?"

"Well, yes. I never had anything designed especially for me, if that's what you mean. But, you see—"

"That," interrupted Madame Moisant firmly, "is exactly what I mean. And that, *mademoiselle,* is the difference between your work and ours. It is no criticism, you understand, of you or your employers...." For a moment an Olympian glanced condescendingly at the well-meant efforts of mere mortals. "But you are under a misapprehension with regard to the work and purpose of a model in a great fashion house."

"A-am I?" Marianne wrinkled her smooth forehead doubtfully, but her clear, beautifully gray eyes looked alert and inquiring, as though even disappointment could not dim her interest in an intriguing discovery.

"You are not alone in that," the Frenchwoman told her with a dry smile. "Many people suppose that the sole business of a model is to look beautiful, walk gracefully and display an outfit to the best advantage. But in a great dress house, these considerations are secondary. Hundreds—probably thousands—of good-looking girls can do that. The true purpose of a model employed by a designer such as Florian is, above all and beyond all, to inspire him to fresh design."

Madame Moisant paused, with a perfect sense of timing. Then she added, with simple and devastating candor, "You, *mademoiselle,* are not the type to inspire."

For a moment Marianne was silent. Partly from chagrin at being classed as uninspiring, but mostly from the conviction that this time she had been presented with a legitimate and unanswerable argument. Then curiosity got the better of even bitter disappointment, and she asked, on a note of humble inquiry, "Just why would I not 'inspire' anyone, *madame*?"

"Because," returned the Frenchwoman unhesitatingly, "you are, in the nicest sense of the word, ordinary."

"I...see."

"You are charming, pretty, well-groomed, graceful." Inexplicably, she contrived to make these attributes sound slightly less than complimentary. "To inspire a great designer one must be unusual, provocative, possibly even interestingly ugly. You are nonetheless charming because you are none of these, *mademoiselle*. But the plain fact is that neither Florian nor any lesser designer—" in her estimation there were obviously only lesser ones "—would ever look at you and think, '*Mon Dieu*, from this strange and lovely creature a new idea begins to grow.'"

"No," conceded Marianne honestly, "I suppose that's true. I think I see what you mean."

"*Bon*," observed Madame Moisant, who liked people to see what she meant. "It happens sometimes quite suddenly, this awareness that a new type arrives. Only three weeks ago, a girl came up those stairs—" With a reminiscent gleam in her shrewd black eyes, the director gestured toward the curtains that shut off her office from the rest of the great fashion house.

"She was wearing a coat that *hurt*—" Madame Moisant closed her eyes as though in recollection of the anguish that the coat had inspired "—and incredibly, cotton gloves. But—" she sucked in her breath in remembered excitement "—her cheekbones! And the curious slant of the eyes! I asked her to wait a moment, and I sent for Monsieur Florian on some pretext or other...."

She paused so long this time, in the interests of drama, that Marianne felt impelled to ask, "What did he say when he saw her?"

"He said, 'When can you start?'" replied Madame Moisant, with telling simplicity. Then she folded and handed back Marianne's references. "Thank you, *mademoiselle*. It has been pleasant to meet you."

The interview was so obviously at an end that Marianne was forced to her feet, still lost in envious contemplation of the good fortune bestowed on the girl with the remarkable cheekbones and slanting eyes. But even then she could not forbear a final appeal.

"*Madame*," she said, "I won't press my claims as a model further. You've convinced me of my unsuitability. But isn't there *any* other way in which I might work here? I've had varied selling experience and—I know it may sound silly and sentimental—but for two years it has been my dream and ambition to work in Paris. That's why I've perfected my French and tried so hard to—''

"There are other fashion houses in Paris," observed Madame Moisant, though in a tone that relegated them to comparative insignificance.

"But only one Florian," countered Marianne quickly.

"True," agreed the Frenchwoman, complacently but unhelpfully.

And then, as she said this, the silver gray curtains parted unexpectedly and a man came into the room. He was not handsome. He was not even especially young. But he carried with him an air of such easy authority that, even without the suddenly attentive air of Madame Moisant, Marianne would have known this was the great Florian himself.

She expected him to brush her and her small affairs from his path. But instead, what he said to his director with a faint, half-sarcastic smile was, "Come, Suzanne, be a little more cooperative—'' evidently he was on very good terms with her "—wholehearted devotion is not to be met with every day. What is it that *mademoiselle* wants?''

"The usual." Madame Moisant shrugged disparagingly.

But Marianne knew suddenly that opportunity was knocking at her door, and metaphorically speaking, she flung that door wide.

"I had hoped there might be a chance of my being taken on as a model, *monsieur*," she said quickly. "But *madame la directrice* has at least convinced me that that is impossible.''

"Indeed?" Florian looked genuinely curious. "How did she do that?''

"She said I was too ordinary to inspire any designer, and I think she is probably right," Marianne stated, without rancor and without false modesty. "But I still dare to hope there may be a place for me here. I do

know a good deal about fashion, *monsieur*, and I can
sell anything.''

"Such as?''

"The right hat to make a woman feel her best,
the right handbag to make a simple suit look expensive,
and the right gloves to make a social climber look a
lady.''

Immediately a subtle increase of interest showed on
Florian's clever, worn face.

"Well,'' he said good-humoredly, "those are no
mean claims, if you can make them good.''

"She is too young for a *vendeuse* in the salon,''
Madame Moisant interposed warningly.

"She is, however, the right age to impart gaiety and
élan to the boutique,'' retorted Florian. "How old are
you, *mademoiselle*?''

"Twenty-two.''

"You look younger. Any family?''

"Why—yes.'' Marianne was faintly surprised to be
asked anything so personal. "I'm the second in a family
of four. The others live at home with my parents in London.''

"And have your parents any objection to your working in Paris?''

"No, *monsieur*. Would it have mattered if they
had?''

"It might. Paris is the Mecca of starry-eyed, ambitious daughters. And once I have begun to train someone, it is both boring and irritating to have indignant
parents trying to summon her home.''

Marianne smiled.

"My parents will not be indignant,'' she promised.
"Nor will they try to summon me home.'' And her heart
began to beat hopefully, for surely Florian would not
ask all these questions if he had no intention of even
considering her.

"Would you—would you care to see my references,
monsieur?'' she asked almost timidly, remembering
Madame Moisant's cavalier reception of them.

"If you please." He held out a remarkably beautiful hand for them, and added, "Sit down again, *mademoiselle*."

So Marianne sat down once more, and held her breath while Florian leaned carelessly against the desk and studied the glowing statements that her late firm had made about her.

"They seem to think well of you," he observed when he had read them. "And now you want to prove yourself in Paris, eh?"

"Yes, *monsieur*. If you would be so good—so kind—"

"I am neither good nor kind, as Madame Moisant here will tell you," Florian informed her dryly. "I am a hard businessman, with a flair for picking my staff and extracting the last ounce of value from them. But I have an idea—" he studied her with an impersonal attention that was slightly disconcerting "—that you are the girl I have been waiting for for sometime. From a business point of view, of course," he added with a faint smile.

"R-really, *monsieur*?" After Madame Moisant's disparaging remarks, this was balm.

"You are determined without being offensive, I notice, and you're quick to seize an opportunity. Also, you have a proper appreciation of your own qualities, which is something quite different from conceit, and very necessary in this world, where the meek go to the wall and stay there."

"The same can be said of many girls," put in Madame Moisant rather crossly. "You speak only of minimum essentials."

"True," agreed Florian calmly. "But *mademoiselle* possesses also dignity without dullness, style without affectation and, above all, that indefinable something that one can only call 'quality.' The British tend to have it more often than most, I have noticed," he added reflectively.

"Monsieur Florian, you—you overwhelm me," exclaimed Marianne.

"Not at all, *mademoiselle*," Florian returned coolly.

"I merely state facts. These qualities you have. But if I find you do not employ them as I require, they are useless to me and you no longer interest me. I must warn you that, if you work here, the House of Florian must be your first concern. Which prompts me to ask one final question. Have you a fiancé?"

"No-no, *monsieur*."

He sighed impatiently.

"Well, what is the complication?" he inquired.

"The—complication, *monsieur*?"

"Yes. There was a slight hesitation before your 'No.' Which means one of three things: either you are engaged but wish to hide the fact, or you are not engaged but wish you were, or you were once engaged and feel nostalgic about it. All of these circumstances could occupy your attention to the detriment of your work, so I had better know the situation now."

Marianne laughed a little vexedly.

"Monsieur Florian, I am not engaged, I have never been engaged, and I have no immediate prospect of becoming engaged. With that I think you must be satisfied," she said firmly.

"So?" He stared at her for a moment with those cold, uncomfortably observant gray eyes. Then suddenly he smiled—a singularly attractive smile—and said, "Perhaps even an employer has no right to ask more. When can you begin work in the boutique downstairs, *mademoiselle*?"

For a moment Marianne could not believe that he had uttered the magic words for which she had been envying another girl only ten minutes earlier. But then she pulled herself together and said eagerly, "Whenever you say, Monsieur Florian. Next week—tomorrow—now, if you like."

"Now is a little too early," he said, again with that slight smile. "But tomorrow would be good. The new collection goes on show less than two weeks from today, and the sooner you are familiar with the boutique, the better. In this firm, it plays an important part. Madame Moisant, arrange the terms of *mademoiselle's* employment. Then take her around and show her whatever you think advisable. She is engaged. What is your name, by the way, *mademoiselle*?''

"M-Marianne, *monsieur*. Marianne Shore.''

"Marianne?'' He repeated the name reflectively. "It is charming—and suitable.''

And, apparently having decided to leave whatever other matter had brought him into the room until later, Florian made a slight gesture of farewell and went away.

"You are a fortunate girl,'' observed Madame Moisant severely.

"Oh, I know it!'' Marianne said fervently.

"It is as well. But now,'' went on the director, "it will be necessary to prove yourself. Monsieur Florian's standards are high. Many people,'' she added, in case Marianne should be getting any inflated ideas of her own worthiness, "find them unattainable. But—we will see how you shape up. First we will talk business, and then I will take you around.''

Necessary though it was to be realistic about her living expenses, Marianne would have said yes to everything, even if the terms had been less generous. As it was, although Madame Moisant assured her dryly that she would be expected to earn every centime of her salary, she felt she was being very fairly treated.

And then, in a haze of happiness and relief, she followed Madame Moisant from the office, deliciously aware that she was no longer a visitor on sufferance but a member of the staff.

Marianne had been long enough in the fashion world to have shed most of the more popular illusions. She knew, for instance, that what the outside world characterized as "glamour'' was merely the dazzling final result of grueling work, endless patience and rigid discipline. And she knew that what appeared to be an elegant and leisurely display of sweetness and beauty often screened crises and heartburning behind the scenes.

But the crowded workrooms were new to her, with

their hundreds of girls—they were all girls, Madame Moisant informed her, whether sixteen or sixty—stitching away for dear life on ravishing materials. From the humblest junior scuttling about picking up pins, to the most exalted fitter intent on hairline exactness, everyone was working with almost ferocious absorption.

Matching, tucking, ruching, pressing, humbly hemming or ambitiously embroidering, with the delicacy of artists, on exquisite flounces and panels. The hum of conversation was unceasing, but hardly anyone looked up from her work, even when the director passed.

From the workrooms Madame Moisant took Marianne through one or two of the unexpectedly small fitting rooms to the great salon itself—empty now, but magically evocative of fantastic fashion shows. With its silver gray curtains, its faintly flushed lights, its delicate paneling and its almost decadently luxurious carpet, it seemed to be waiting in a sort of insolent languor for the inevitable moment when it would come to life and justify its existence, as the perfect shell in which the shimmering pearls of the fashion world would be displayed.

Down the center of the long room ran the inevitable raised platform, ending in the small circular stage on which the models would execute their final pirouettes before disappearing through the curtains into the dressing room beyond. Madame Moisant now took Marianne through these curtains, observing as she did so, "It is, of course, the dead season now, so far as fashion shows are concerned. Most of the girls are upstairs being fitted."

One or two, however, were lounging in the dressing room, either sitting with their feet up or studying their reflections in the long wall mirror, while they changed a hairstyle or altered their makeup.

"This is Mademoiselle Marianne," Madame Moisant informed them *en bloc*. "She will be working in the boutique."

One or two of them returned Marianne's comprehensive smile with a flicker of greeting. But she had the curious impression that, for them at this moment, only a fellow model would really impinge on their consciousness.

As they turned to go, Madame Moisant paused beside a girl whose incredibly beautiful red gold head was bent over a fashion magazine.

"This," she said to Marianne, "is Lisette, of whom I told you earlier."

At the mention of her name, the girl raised her head, and Marianne saw instantly that here were the cheekbones and the slanting eyes that had earned Monsieur Florian's immediate interest.

It was understandable, she thought. For not only was the bone structure of the face flawless, the lovely slanting eyes were of a clear, translucent green, in strange, intriguing contrast to the red, faintly sensual mouth. The girl could not have been more than twenty, but the enigmatic expression of those eyes seemed to hide the knowledge of the ages. Even so might some exquisite cat goddess of ancient times have looked upon her adorers. Cool and completely inscrutable.

But what the cat goddess said, in a charming, throaty sort of voice, was, "Hello. You're English, aren't you?"

"Yes, I'm English." Marianne smiled at her. "Are you?"

"No. My mother was English, but my father came from the Levant, and I myself was born in Athens."

"Your English is perfect," Marianne told her admiringly.

"Yes, I know." She accepted that as her due. "So are my French and my Greek."

"How wonderful to have three languages," Marianne said sincerely.

"It's better to have slanting eyes," said the cat goddess succinctly, and she went back to her fashion magazine.

Outside the dressing-room door, Marianne laughed a little and said to Madame Moisant, "Now I see exactly what you mean. She made me feel ordinary indeed. She's quite wonderful looking, isn't she?"

"She is also, if I am not mistaken, a man-eater," replied Madame Moisant, on a note of calm reflection.

"A—a man-eater?"

"Yes. She does not care for her own sex, that little one. She likes to make men mad about her. Well, that is not our concern. So long as she does not try to eat the man of some rich customer, of course. It is possible that we shall have trouble with her."

But Madame Moisant seemed to view that prospect with equanimity, and after a moment she went on, in a mood of unusual expansiveness, "Most of the girls are hard working, ambitious, and rather stupid. This is very good, for then they do what they are told, and Monsieur Florian—and I—" she added in modest parenthesis, "know exactly what is best for them. But sometimes, when the other qualities are too good to ignore, one has to take an intelligent one. Lisette, I think, is intelligent. It is a pity, but—" she shrugged "—one must not ask too much of heaven. With such cheekbones and eyes, one must suffer the rest. Now I will take you to the boutique and introduce you to Madame Rachel who is in charge...there."

The small but significant pause before the last word was enough to tell Marianne that Madame Rachel's authority was not allowed to trespass in the smallest degree into the realm of Madame Moisant. And when, a few minutes later, she was taken into the boutique and presented to the elegant, gray-haired woman who ruled there, she understood the situation exactly.

The impeccable and distant politeness with which the two ladies conducted themselves toward each other was more telling than if they had shrieked their rivalry aloud. And when Madame Moisant sought to explain Marianne's presence, Madame Rachel interrupted, with all the sweetness and chill of high-class ice cream, to say that Monsieur Florian had already been to see her personally and had explained all.

Sensible man, thought Marianne amusedly, and

stepped aside to allow the passage of a tall, good-looking man who had just entered but seemed a trifle out of place in the exquisite surroundings of the boutique.

"Monsieur Senloe!" cried both the Frenchwomen in chorus. And Madame Moisant added, in her heavily accented English, "Monsieur Florian will be delighted. We hardly expected you in Paris this season."

"I hardly expected it myself until yesterday," was the good-humored reply, delivered in the unmistakable accent of Great Britain. "Is Monsieur Florian free? Or...."

"But of course—for you. Please come—" and Madame Moisant wafted the visitor up the gray carpeted stairs before Madame Rachel could insert so much as a word on her own account.

Something told Marianne that to assume a degree of special knowledge on Madame Rachel's part would, at this moment, be soothing to that lady's pride. So she said, "Is Mr. Senloe also in the fashion world?"

"*Pas du tout.* He is in the *corps diplomatique.*" Madame Rachel spoke with a touch of graciousness very acceptable after the astringent asperity of Madame Moisant. "He is a very good friend of Monsieur Florian. He nearly married Madame Florian," she added somewhat irrelevantly, Marianne could not help thinking.

Feeling that this constituted a curious claim on Monsieur Florian's friendship, Marianne said. "But doesn't that make it rather...rather, awkward for them all?"

"Oh, no." Madame Rachel shook her head and smiled, a really lovely smile. "Perhaps he still adores Madame Florian nostalgically. But it was all some years ago now. He was what you English call a good loser. Since then he has become the good friend of them both. He is devoted to Monsieur Florian."

Marianne felt morally certain that the big, good-looking Englishman would have died rather than describe himself as devoted to any of his men friends. But she let that pass, and Madame Rachel added reflectively, "One is always either devoted to Monsieur Florian or wishing him dead. There is no middle way."

And, while Marianne stored away this interesting bit of information about her new employer, Madame Rachel proceeded to show her something of the boutique.

Marianne had at one time worked in the exclusive gift shop of her London store, and she was not quite a stranger to the kind of merchandise displayed in the Florian boutique. But it was all on an even more attractive and intriguing scale than anything she had previously handled.

Here there was no sign of the leisured diplomacy that was required in the salon upstairs. Customers came and went, saw what they wanted almost at a glance and frequently completed their purchases in a matter of minutes. Though some, of course, chose to wander around inspecting, inquiring and comparing.

Scarves and gloves, handbags, a few special cosmetics and a great deal of wonderful costume jewelry made up most of the stock. Though once the new collection went on show, Madame Rachel told her, they would also be selling a certain number of exclusive "separates."

"There is little here at the moment." Madame Rachel shrugged. "But in two weeks—all will be changed."

Like Madame Moisant—like Florian himself—she spoke as though in two weeks' time night would become day, winter would become spring, and the whole world would begin to live again.

"Tomorrow, Mademoiselle Marianne, you shall observe and learn. There are three other *vendeuses* besides yourself. Célestine, who is away this afternoon, Jeanne, who is checking stock, and Marcelle, who is, as you will observe, showing our most expensive handbags to *madame*, who will eventually buy a small *boutonniere*. She wastes time, that one."

But the tone was more indulgent than any Madame Moisant would have used in similar circumstances, Marianne felt sure, and it occurred to her that possibly her life down here in the boutique would be a good deal easier than it could ever have been upstairs.

Presently, realizing that she had occupied as much of Madame Rachel's time as was suitable, she said good-bye, and having promised to be at the boutique in good time in the morning, she stepped out into the crisp, keen air of the late February afternoon.

In almost every season of the year, and almost every hour of the day, Paris has her individual charm for those who love her. And, as Marianne walked up the long slope of the Avenue Marceau, it seemed to her that there was pure magic in the tingling freshness of the air on her cheeks, the first faint curtain of approaching twilight, and the glimmer of the single early star that hung motionless above the Arc de Triomphe.

"I'm the luckiest girl alive," she told herself. "I'm to live here, in Paris. I'm to work for the great Florian, and somewhere in this same enchanted city, Nat is living and working, too."

At last she could bring that wonderful, incredible, glorious fact into the forefront of her mind again. During the last few hours Nat had, perforce, been at the back of her consciousness, though never entirely absent from it. Now she could revel afresh in the knowledge that he was here, in Paris—and all the more so since the events of the afternoon had assured her future here.

Even now it was hard to believe there was no longer anything wrong in thinking of Nat with tenderness and hope, instead of the guilty sense of anguish that had pursued her for months. For, if you are foolish enough—or unfortunate enough—to fall in love with your sister's fiancé, what can you do but struggle to hide your remorseful heartache behind a casual, friendly manner?

It was not as though she had ever been anything but deeply fond of Yvonne, who was the nicest and gayest of elder sisters. That was what had made it so awful when she had found herself falling for the thin, dark, vivid charm of Nat Gilmore.

And then, as though that were not enough, when

Yvonne's somewhat erratic hours at the television studio impelled her to break an evening engagement with her fiancé, the most natural solution to everyone appeared to be that Marianne should accompany him instead to whatever play or film he had to review for the newspaper on which he worked.

She had both treasured and dreaded those evenings with Nat. For, although she enjoyed every perilous moment of them, she knew quite well that she was playing with the most dangerous fire.

Nat was completely unaware of all this, she knew. He was in no way a philanderer, and would probably have been embarrassed and appalled if he had guessed that his fiancée's younger sister adored him. Instead, he treated her with an easy, good-humored affection, and made her the safe recipient of his occasional grumbles whenever he considered that Yvonne put the interest of her work too obviously before the interests of himself.

And all this had gone on for more months than Marianne cared to remember.

When she had told Madame Moisant that for two years she had dreamed of working in Paris, this was true. For it was at least two years since she had first had the exciting idea. Unquestionably that ambition had faltered during the early days of her devotion to Nat. But common sense had finally brought her to the realization that in her Paris plan lay the solution to her unhappy dilemma.

So, steeling herself to the painful decision, Marianne had announced her intention of leaving her London job, allowing herself two or three weeks' winter holiday in Paris—to get the feel of life there and to perfect her already very serviceable French—and then to trying her luck with one of the big fashion houses, preferably Florian's.

Her parents had raised no objection, and it had occurred to Marianne that possibly her mother at least suspected something of her younger daughter's problem. Yvonne had pronounced it a wonderful idea, and her two young brothers, Henry and Basil, had both approved the plan, on the principle that a sister in Paris could be very useful, especially during school holidays.

Unexpectedly, it had been Nat who had made the only energetic protest, and his frank dismay had pierced her heart.

"Why, Marianne, what can you do in Paris that you can't do equally well here?" he had demanded. "And anyway, to be completely selfish—what am I going to do without you?"

"You'll manage very well," she told him, with a cheerful callousness she was far from feeling. "And you'll see a lot more of Yvonne. If I'm not there to fill the gap usefully, she'll have to make herself more easily available. Perhaps I've been around just a little too much in the last few months."

"You couldn't be," he told her quite simply. And those were the three meager words that Marianne clung to for comfort when she finally made the agonizing break.

Paris enchanted her from the very first day. All the same, whenever a letter arrived from her mother—the only reliable correspondent in the family—she searched it eagerly for even a passing reference to Nat. But she searched it in vain. Possibly her mother thought he was a subject best left alone. Even her references to Yvonne seemed unnecessarily sketchy.

Then, only that morning, a letter had come from Yvonne herself. And even now, as she walked along the crowded Paris pavement in the deepening twilight, with the golden street lamps beginning to twinkle through the leafless branches of the trees, Marianne caught her breath afresh at the realization of how that letter had changed her life.

Yvonne had written:

I ought to have written to you earlier, but things have been rather difficult. And now I'd better tell you right away what has happened. Nat and I have decided we can't make a go of it. There wasn't any terrific quarrel or anything like that, and, although

I'm a bit blue, it's no good pretending that I'm shattered—which just goes to show he was never the right man for me. The fact is that I just love my work—and possibly my boss—better than Nat.

I hope he doesn't feel too badly about it. I don't *think* he does, for he made no protest when I told him how I felt. He just said quietly that he wasn't entirely surprised, and that if the break had to come, this was the best time for it, as he had been posted to Paris by the paper, and expected to be away at least three months.

I couldn't help thinking that Paris was rather providential, as you are there. And I shouldn't be surprised if you find yourself playing your familiar role of comforter in my absence. Be nice to him if you do run into him, Marianne. Or perhaps you have run into him already, for all this happened ten days ago! He's rather a darling. Only he's not *my* darling.

Be nice to him! Be nice to him! In the whole wide world there was nothing Marianne wanted more than the chance—the right—to "be nice" to Nat, and she hardly knew whether to laugh aloud or to sit down and cry when she read her sister's airy injunction.

What she did do, since she was practical as well as romantic, was to decide that this was the day on which she would go out and find herself a job. For if Nat were to be working in Paris during the next few months, then Marianne was going to be there, too, if she had to sweep streets in order to do so.

This, then, explained her resolute determination in the face of Madame Moisant's attempted rejection of her. And this also explained the lightness of her step and the irrepressible smile on her lips as she walked homeward now through Paris to her modest pension.

If she were to stay in Paris indefinitely, Marianne supposed she would eventually want to find a small apartment, or at least a room, of her own. But for the time being she was well satisfied with a reasonably large

attic bedroom in a tall, old-fashioned house where bed
and breakfast were provided for students and others of
limited means.

It was no hardship to her to have to go out for her main
meals. On the contrary, she loved exploring, and she had
already found one or two places where, in unpretentious
surroundings, one could eat remarkably well.

Tonight, however, she thought, as she changed in her
bedroom under the eaves, called for something in the
nature of a celebration. She would go somewhere special. But where?

And then, as though by inspiration, she recalled hearing one of the more prosperous students refer to a particularly attractive restaurant, which he described as
"just across the water from Notre Dame."

"Writers and people like that go there," he said. "It's
quite a favorite haunt of foreign journalists. Not a
tourists' stamping ground, but the kind of place recommended to each other by people in the know."

Was it conceivable that someone "in the know" had
already recommended it to Nat? Might he not be one of
the foreign journalists who went there?

In her mind's eye she already saw him sitting alone at
one of the tables. And then she came in and went up to
him and just said "Hello, Nat!" And that was the most
wonderful moment in an utterly wonderful day.

Indeed, there was something so right about it, so entirely in keeping with the pattern of this incredible day,
that Marianne suddenly knew that she was going to see
him there. It was as though something or someone outside herself assured her of the fact.

And so, later, when she judged it was about the right
time to find Nat having his evening meal, she ran all the
way down the four flights of stairs from her attic room,
and out into the enchanted streets once more. Here
she allowed herself the unusual extravagance of a taxi.
And, after a breathtaking and somewhat terrifying ten
minutes, she found herself set down before a rather
more intimidatingly handsome place than she had expected.

However, with the curious conviction still upon her that it was here she would meet Nat again, she pushed open the door and stepped boldly inside.

The place was already more than half-full, but it did not take her more than a few moments to realize that Nat was not there. Even so, she told herself with certainty that he would come and, when a waiter approached her to show her to a table, she said, "I'll sit here near the door. I'm expecting someone."

She did not order her meal immediately, but sat there sipping a glass of wine and absently breaking and eating pieces of crusty bread. Then, after a while, the first faint chill crept over her and she thought bewilderedly, *what am I doing? I'm perfectly mad, sitting here waiting for Nat to walk in. Why should he? There are dozens—hundreds—of other places where he's just as likely to be. The odds against our choosing the same place are tremendous.*

At this point she summoned her waiter and ordered her meal, telling herself that she would simply enjoy a quiet little celebration on her own. But she was glad that the meal seemed likely to take some while, and still her glance turned eagerly, hopefully toward the door every time it swung open.

Inevitably, her earlier mood of elation had cooled, but in spite of all the arguments she recited to herself, she was not really convinced of failure. And when, for the twentieth time, the door swung open and she saw Nat standing there, narrowing his dark eyes for a moment against the sudden bright lights, she almost cried aloud, *"I knew it!"*

Then he moved forward, and with a sense of indescribable shock she realized that he was not alone.

It was so totally unexpected, so different from anything she had planned or foreseen, that for a second she hardly took in his companion as an individual at all. Then suddenly everything seemed to shift into focus again. And, with a chill sense of dismay like nothing else she had ever known, she recognized the red gold hair and the slanting green eyes of Lisette.

So complete and numbing was the shock that she could only sit there and stare. Then, when she realized that they had passed—that *Nat* had passed within a few yards of her without even noticing she was there—it seemed to her that she actually heard her world crumbling.

At that most inappropriate moment the waiter arrived with her meal.

"Oh, no! I couldn't eat anything. I—I must go," stammered Marianne, aware of nothing but the urgency of flight.

"But, *madame*...." The astonished waiter paused, undecided. "Are you ill?"

She thought of saying yes. Then she was afraid that might cause a stir that could conceivably draw Nat's attention. The last thing in the world that she wanted at this moment.

"It isn't that," she managed to say calmly. "I've just suddenly remembered a terribly urgent appointment. I can't think how I forgot. Please bring me my bill—quickly. I'll pay for the meal, of course. But I must go—I must go."

There was no arguing with that note of desperation, and the waiter began to make out the bill, with all speed.

Even so, the delay seemed interminable to Marianne, who sat there with her head bent, nervously crumbling a piece of bread while she prayed confusedly that she might escape recognition for a few moments longer.

Only five minutes ago she had longed, more than anything else in the world, to hear Nat's surprised voice exclaim, "Why—Marianne!" Now she thought she would die of shame if he—and that girl—discovered her sitting there. She had the dreadful conviction that if Nat spoke to her now, the tears of shock and disappointment would become uncontrollable, and she would somehow betray to both of them the absurd and pitiable reason for her presence there. All she wanted was to get away—to get away.

At last the bill was made out and paid. And reaching for her coat, she slid into it with as little fuss as possible and almost literally fled from the place that she had visualized as the scene of joyful reunion. Instead—instead....

She walked rapidly, not caring where she was going, so long as she kept away from any brightly lighted streets. And presently, finding herself near a seat on a quiet stretch of the riverbank, she sat down uncaring of the cold, and tried to bring some sort of order into the desperate confusion of her thoughts and emotions.

Clutching at some remnants of common sense, she told herself that she was making the most ridiculous fuss about very little. Disappointment was understandable, but—why shouldn't Lisette go out for a casual dinner engagement with an English journalist she might have chanced to meet? And Nat was bound to know heaps of people in his job. Why not Lisette?

It was unspeakably chilling to have Nat walk past her without even seeing her, of course. Only he had no idea of her presence in the restaurant, so was it so strange that he should fail to notice her?

Marianne repeated these sensible arguments to herself. But they were just words. Hollow, hollow words, which carried not the faintest hint of consolation. The only thing that was certain and inescapable was that the glorious day had turned into an evening of mockery.

If it had not been Lisette, she would not have been so frightened and dismayed. With something like a shock, Marianne realized this without being able to explain just why. But—it had been Lisette. And like a picture on a screen, the scene seemed to unroll itself before her again. The lovely, enigmatic redhead walking past with Nat, while she, Marianne, could only sit there and watch.

She heard herself give a slight sob at the recollection. And suddenly she found the tears were pouring down her cheeks in a shaming, horrifying flood. Panic-stricken, she fumbled for her handkerchief while she heard another of those irrepressible sobs.

She couldn't possibly go on like this, she told herself. But she went on.

And then, suddenly, an unmistakably English voice said, "Excuse me if this isn't my business. But—can I do anything to help?"

Feeling that this was the ultimate in shame, Marianne looked up through her tears and saw standing before her the tall, good-looking Englishman who had come into the boutique that afternoon.

CHAPTER TWO

"OH," GASPED MARIANNE. "How awful! You must think me a perfect fool, but—but...."

"I don't think you anything of the sort," the man said kindly. "Everyone feels that way once in a while, I suppose. But if there's something seriously wrong...." He paused and regarded her with a touch of genuine concern. "You're English, aren't you?"

Marianne nodded.

"And I've seen you somewhere quite recently."

She hung her head, not really wishing to be recognized by anyone connected with the place where she was going to work.

"I know," he exclaimed suddenly. "You were in Florian's boutique this afternoon, weren't you?"

"Y-yes. But how could you possibly remember? You only saw me for a moment."

"Photographic memory," he assured her with a grin. "And don't be cross with me for it. People who possess the gift rather pride themselves upon the fact. It's like being able to raise one eyebrow without the other, or wiggle your ears. It makes you feel exclusive."

She laughed faintly at that, and he said, "That's better. Do you want me to walk on now and mind my own business, or may I sit down and hear if there's anything I can do to help?"

"There's nothing anyone can do to help," she said with a sigh. But instinctively she made room for him on the bench beside her.

"That's hardly ever strictly true, you know," he told her consolingly. "Practically every problem has some sort of answer. And they usually fall into one of two categories. Shall I guess?"

"No-no. At least—" she glanced at him curiously "—you *can't* guess, can you?"

"You'd be surprised." He smiled at her, and his unusually bright eyes crinkled attractively at the corners. "Let me see. You're scared because you're broke and in a foreign country, and although you've tried for a job—possibly even at Florian's—you can't get one. And you don't know what on earth to do next."

Again she gave that faint laugh, because it was not possible to feel quite so awful about things when he reviewed the position so cheerfully.

"No. You're wrong, as a matter of fact. I did badly want a job in Paris, it's true. But this afternoon I got one—almost the ideal one. I'm to work in Florian's boutique."

"Are you really?" He looked interested. "Well, that should be a reasonably paying job, so your trouble can't be financial."

"N-no." She shook her head and looked down at her tightly clasped hands.

There was a slight silence. Then he said kindly, "Has he gone off with someone else?"

"Wh-what?" She looked up, so startled by his perception that she was almost frightened.

"Don't look so scared. It wasn't awfully difficult to guess. It's always either love or fear that makes one think the bottom's dropped out of the world. And I know how you're feeling. It happened to me once—"

"Oh, yes, of course!" Suddenly she remembered Madame Rachel's somewhat indiscreet disclosure.

"What do you mean—'oh, yes, of course'?" He looked taken aback in his turn.

"She married Florian instead of you, didn't she?" said Marianne before she could stop herself. "Oh, I'm—terribly sorry!" She clapped her hand over her mouth a moment too late.

He looked rather quizzical.

"As a matter of fact, she did," he replied dryly. "But how did you know? Does Florian boast of his success to casual callers?"

"Oh, *no!*" Marianne was quite horrified at this picture of her imperturbable employer, even if it was hardly offered seriously. "No, it was just—oh, dear, this is going to sound dreadfully gossipy, I'm afraid—"

"Boutiques are hotbeds of gossip," he assured her, still in that dry tone of voice.

"I—remarked on you, after you had gone upstairs. Asked if you were in the fashion world or—"

"Good Lord! Do I *look* as though I am?"

"Not in the least," Marianne hastened to assure him. "That was why I was curious, I expect. Anyway, someone said you were a great friend of the Florians. And—and then added the information that you...nearly married Madame Florian."

"So much for the naive belief that one's private affairs can remain one's own," he observed with a slight grimace.

"I'm terribly sorry. I had no right to make such a remark." Marianne spoke with real contrition. "I wouldn't have, I'm sure, if we hadn't started to talk in this extraordinarily frank way."

"Well, it hasn't been one-sided," he agreed with a good-tempered little laugh and shrug. "I rather asked for it by questioning you so closely—"

"Oh, but you meant it so kindly," Marianne interrupted quickly. "I—I'm glad you did."

"Are you really?" He looked amused, but touched. "Look here, why don't we go somewhere a bit warmer to finish this conversation? Come and have a meal with me—or have you already dined?"

"N-no," said Marianne, wincing as she recalled the dreadful moment when she had sent away the meal she had ordered. "I haven't had anything to eat. But I don't think—I mean, I didn't think—"

"You didn't think you'd ever be able to eat anything again," he amplified for her knowledgeably. "But now you're beginning to feel shamefully hungry, in spite of a broken heart."

She laughed, in spite of herself. "How did you know?"

"By observing human nature for more years than I'm
going to tell you. Let me see—" he glanced around
"—there's quite a good place not so far from here. The
average tourist hasn't found it yet. But it's a favorite
with foreign journalists and diplomats and—"

"Oh, no!" exclaimed Marianne before he could get
any further. "Do you mean the Secret de Polichinelle?"

"That's the place. Don't you like it? I thought—"

"It isn't that." She hesitated. Then, unable to stop
herself, she blurted out, "He's there now. With—with
another girl. That's why I came away."

"Oh, Lord, I am sorry!"

"No—it's all right. You couldn't possibly know.
Only it's almost uncanny that you should suggest the
same place."

"Not really, you know. Foreign visitors of a certain
type tend to gravitate to the same places in any city. And
journalists and minor diplomats always know the same
spots. But of course we'll go somewhere else, in quite
another district."

And raising his hand, he summoned a passing taxi
and helped her in.

She paid no attention to the directions he gave. They
hardly mattered. She only knew that he had promised to
take her right away from the place where Nat was possibly now looking into Lisette's green eyes—and she felt
instinctively that she could leave the rest to him.

"By the way, it's about time I introduced myself," he
said, as they drove through the lamplit streets into a
much gayer part of the city. "My name's Roger
Senloe."

"And mine is Marianne Shore. But, in a way, I'd
almost like you to—to forget all about me, once this
evening's over."

"I should find that extraordinarily difficult to do,"
he told her gravely. "But if you mean will I please keep
my mouth shut about everything you've said, I give you
my word on that."

"Thank you. It's not that my little affairs are of any
special importance or interest," she admitted humbly.

"But you know Monsieur Florian, and I'm going to work there, and if you told him about this, as a piquant story—"

"I never tell Florian piquant stories," he assured her solemnly. "For one thing, our views on piquancy differ quite a lot. And anyway, remember that if your secret is partially mine, my secret is entirely yours." And he turned his head and smiled at her mischievously.

"Oh, well—yes. I suppose that's true." She found herself smiling in return. "Though of course I wouldn't dream of saying anything about that. And anyway—" she glanced at him diffidently, but with real interest "—suppose Monsieur Florian knows—about you?"

"Monsieur Florian tends to know about most things," Roger Senloe conceded. "I see no reason to suppose that I and my affairs constitute an exception."

At this point they arrived at the restaurant he had chosen in preference to the Secret de Polichinelle, and Marianne privately gave him full marks for the fact that it could hardly have been more different from the one she had left an hour ago. Small, unpretentious and homely, with checked cloths on the tables, it proved all the same to supply superb food. And she felt herself insensibly relax in the friendly atmosphere.

He went to some trouble to see that she had exactly what she wanted. But it was not until they were idling pleasantly over the delicious coffee that he said, "Feeling better now?"

"Yes, thank you. Heaps better. In fact—" mentally she surveyed the situation afresh and was a little surprised to find she had previously viewed it in such a tragic light "—I'm not sure," she said slowly, "that I haven't made a ridiculous amount of fuss about very little."

"One sometimes does." He sounded comfortingly matter-of-fact. "It's extraordinarily difficult to be objective and levelheaded where one's deepest feelings are concerned. But you excite my curiosity afresh, and I can't help asking—did he deliberately stand you up for someone else?''

"Oh—no! He didn't even know I was there."

"Didn't know you were there?" Her companion looked astonished. Perhaps understandably so.

"It was just that I'd so hoped—I was so sure—"

And then, unable to stop herself, Marianne found the words tumbling out, and she was explaining to him all about the months when she had loved Nat, but had had to stand aside and watch him as the fiancé of her sister. With a frankness she would not have believed possible, she told him how she had felt when Yvonne's letter had come that morning.

The only things she kept back were the actual names. She told him how hope had flared sky-high, how she had made her position secure by finding work at Florian's, and then how the absolute conviction had come upon her that, if she went to a certain restaurant, she would see him there.

"And I was right. The instinct *was* right. It was all exactly as it should have been. Only—he came with another girl." And, at the recollection of that awful moment of disillusionment, she stared down bleakly into her coffee cup.

He had listened attentively to her rapidly told tale. And, now that her voice had trailed off into silence, he actually patted her hand with long, strong fingers.

"I do see it must have been a frightful shock," he said. "But the implications are not all that tragic, you know. It's only ten days since he was turned down by his fiancée; he can't have had much time to get seriously involved with anyone else."

"N-no. That's true."

"On the other hand, a man feels pretty much at loose ends after an experience of that sort. What is more natural than that he should find a pleasant companion and go out for the evening?"

It all sounded quite logical, put like that. But—

"It's odd, that, that he didn't try to get in touch with

me. He knew I was in Paris. And we—we so often went out together.''

"Perhaps he felt a bit self-conscious about you, since it was your sister who ditched him,'' Roger Senloe suggested.

"Well, yes. I suppose that could be so. In fact—yes, of course, that must be so!'' She was surprised now that she had not thought of this before, and the simple explanation of his silence appealed to her as immeasurably cheering.

"Oh, I'm so glad I met you!'' she exclaimed impulsively. "You've made me feel quite differently about things.''

"Have I? Well, that's fine, and I'm glad we met each other, too. I hope you didn't mean it too literally when you said a while ago that you wanted me to forget all about you after this evening.''

"Not—too literally perhaps. Anyway—'' she smiled "—you know where to find me.''

"Of course! At Florian's. When do you start work?''

"Tomorrow morning.''

"Tomorrow, eh?'' He glanced at his watch. "Then I suggest I take you home now. You'll have to make quite an early start, if I know the rules there. And you'll need to feel your best for the demands of a first day.''

He called the waiter, paid the bill and had a taxi summoned.

At this point, Marianne tried to assure him that she could manage on her own, but he would have none of it.

"No, no. We'll complete the evening properly,'' he told her. And not until they were outside the high, old-fashioned house where she lodged did he finally bid her good-night.

"I simply don't know how to thank you,'' she said, holding his hand tightly. "It wasn't just the lovely dinner and—and the talk and everything. It was the way you minded about my being unhappy, even though I was a complete stranger. I expect one day—'' she took an unexpectedly wise glimpse into the future "—I'll forget how I felt in that horrible restaurant. But I'll never, never forget you or how kind you were.''

''My dear child, you overwhelm me.'' He smiled, but he actually flushed a little, too. ''We'll meet again, I'm sure. But if your affairs progress as you hope, I shan't expect you to have very much time for me or anyone else,'' he added teasingly.

Then, lightly brushing aside any further thanks, he bade her good-night and got back into the taxi. And as Marianne mounted the long, steep stairs to her attic room she could not help thinking that if Madame Florian had really turned down that nice man in favor of Florian, either she must be singularly lacking in judgment or Florian must be full of hidden depths she had not yet plumbed.

THE NEXT MORNING neither the depression of the first half of the evening nor the consolation of the latter half seemed quite so clearly defined. Both inevitably faded before the pleasurable anxiety with which Marianne set forth for her first day at Florian's.

She was nervous, of course. But she was eager, too. And, as she walked along through the bright, chilly winter sunshine, she savored afresh the entrancing fact that she was now part of the fascinating, intricate, inexplicable design that makes up the fashion world of Paris.

At the boutique she was greeted pleasantly but briskly by Madame Rachel, and introduced to her colleagues, Célestine, Jeanne and Marcelle. She judged the first two to be rather older than herself, but they possessed that indefinable elegance and finish that make age immaterial. Marcelle, more her own age, seemed conscientious rather than brilliant, but she might well, Marianne thought shrewdly, prove the easiest to get on with.

As Madame Rachel had promised, it was largely a day of observing and learning. Marianne was fortunate, she knew, to come into the boutique at a time when stock was low in preparation for the tremendous flowering of novelties and exclusive lines that would accompany the

launching of the new collection. She had time, in these
two quiet weeks, to familiarize herself with general
routine and to learn about the new stock before it actually came before an eager and demanding public.

Marianne had not exaggerated when she had told
Florian that she could "sell anything." She was, indeed,
a born saleswoman, with a real and intense enjoyment
in the subtle area of combining respect for a customer's
wishes with the discreet employment of her own knowledge and judgment.

"That was good," Madame Rachel observed unequivocally when, during the early part of the afternoon, she had unobtrusively watched Marianne dealing
with a difficult and undecided customer who had finally
gone away completely satisfied, after spending more
than she had seemed likely to spend at first.

"Thank you, *madame*." Marianne smiled.

"There is nothing hard and fast about your technique, I notice, and this is good, for one must always be
flexible when dealing with people. Also you are not
overburdened with the missionary spirit."

"The missionary spirit, Madame?" Marianne looked
inquiring.

"The determination to convert the customer from her
own view to yours," Madame Rachel explained. "This
is often a temptation when one's taste is good. The little
Marcelle has this fault. She is so earnest and she always
knows what is right. This is not always interesting to the
customer who does not know what is right but knows
what she wants. Friendly advice—this is one thing. The
earnest lecture—this is something quite else. But these
things are not to be learned. One either knows them or
not. You, *mademoiselle*, seem to know them."

This unexpectedly early praise delighted Marianne.
And she was just beginning to feel what a delightful
place this was and how happy she was going to be in the
Florian boutique, when an ominous little shadow fell
across the brightness of her mood. For down the stairs
from the salon above came Lisette. And at the sight of
that inscrutable young face beneath the burnished hair,

Marianne felt her heart begin to beat with the remembered anguish of the night before.

"Madame Moisant said that I might come down and ask you about evening bags, *madame*," Lisette explained to the director of the boutique. "She said there might be a little one from last season's stock that would not be too expensive. That possibly, even, there might be one that you would no longer consider suitable for the public and that I might have for nothing."

"Indeed?" Madame Rachel cast an ironical glance over the too casual suppliant. "I am well aware, Lisette, that Madame Moisant would not think of making such an impertinent suggestion, and when you have been here longer you will learn that it does not do to make what the English call the 'try-on' with me. If, however, you mean that you wish to buy an evening bag within your means—taking into account the discount to a member of the firm—then Mademoiselle Marianne will show you some."

Lisette pouted slightly, but made no protestations of innocence. It was perfectly obvious that she had, in Madame Rachel's words, "made the try-on," but as it had failed, she saw no sense in endeavoring to maintain it.

Equally, she was not at all embarrassed at being found out. Smiling faintly, she drifted over to Marianne and stated frankly, "I must have an evening bag. I am going dancing tonight, and I have no bag. Once the new collection goes on show, we shall be modeling and posing for photographers far into the night. There won't be any dancing for me then, so I'm making the most of my time now. Besides—I have a new beau. And he's English, and the English notice details like bags and gloves, don't they?"

For a moment Marianne thought she would not be able to answer at all. Then she cleared her throat and said a trifle huskily that the English did notice such details.

With an immense effort she managed to keep her hands steady as she brought out some of the less expensive bags for Lisette's inspection. And having conquered herself so far, she even managed to ask with the right degree of smiling interest, "Is he very nice, this English beau of yours?"

"Oh, yes." The other girl's attention was almost entirely on the bags, but she switched it for a moment to add, "He is more like a Latin than an Englishman. Dark and vivid and not all solid virtue."

It was on the tip of Marianne's tongue to say indignantly that Nat was intensely British, with most of the solid virtues, even if he did look dark and lively. But with an effort, she controlled herself and asked calmly instead, "Have you known him long?"

"Long enough." The other girl shrugged carelessly. "What is time in these matters?"

Marianne longed to ask quite what she meant by "these matters." But as this was impossible, she searched anxiously in her mind for some other innocuous-sounding question that might elicit a little more information about the situation.

Lisette had now, however—and with great determination—made up her mind about the bag, and she proceeded to try to beat down the price, in a shameless but oddly engaging way.

Marianne glanced over at Madame Rachel with the very slightest raising of her eyebrows. Madame replied with an equally slight shake of her head. So Marianne, pleasantly but with unshakable firmness, indicated that Lisette was wasting her time. And presently Lisette paid for the bag and departed upstairs with it.

"She is not the best element to have in any business," Madame Rachel remarked dryly. "I myself would not have her. But Madame Moisant, of course, knows best," she added, in much the tone Anthony must have used when he described Brutus as an honorable man.

Wisely, Marianne refused to take this up, merely according the remark a noncommittal smile. And presently the long, long first day came to an end.

She made every excuse she could to stay until the last minute, in the hope that Nat would come to collect

Lisette. But once Lisette had drifted out through the
boutique clutching her new bag under her arm, there
was no point in waiting further. She bade her new colleagues good-night and went home—tired by the strain
of her first day, but quite unable to rest for the thought
of Lisette, complete with new bag, dancing out the evening with Nat.

And this, to her mingled dismay and incredulity,
proved to be the pattern of her life during the next ten
days.

She would not have believed it possible that Nat could
be in the same city and yet so completely elusive, or that
she should hear of him—as she did from time to time, in
an indirect sort of way, when Lisette spoke casually of
"her English beau"—and not be able to reach him. But
of whom could she inquire his whereabouts?

Certainly not of Lisette. Presumably not by letter
from anyone at home. For, with the engagement
broken, Nat was hardly likely to remain in contact with
either Yvonne or her mother. She had to wait—and
wait—for him to contact her.

If her work had not been so absorbing, Marianne
would have been in despair, and she was almost glad of
the crescendo of activity, which increased indescribably
as the day of the new fashion show approached.

From the lowest little apprentice to the great man
himself, everyone was nervous, excited, madly optimis-
tic or inordinately depressed, according to temperament
and day-to-day events.

"It's like waiting for a theatrical first night,"
Marianne declared. And Madame Moisant, who happened to be down in the boutique at the time, turned
to her and said coldly, "Only a sensationally important first night can compare with a Florian fashion
show."

"All the same, Marianne has used the right comparison," observed Madame Rachel, who was not going
to have one of her staff put down by her rival. "The
show is in many ways pure theater."

"It is a great deal more than that." Madame Moisant

drew herself up disdainfully. "If you were upstairs, *madame*, you would understand better."

"You forget that I was for many years a *vendeuse* in the salon." Madame Rachel also drew herself up. "There is little I do not know about the madhouse it must be at the moment. How I pity you, *madame*!" And she permitted herself the luxury of a compassionate glance.

"For me, I would not be anywhere else," retorted the other lady angrily. And she flounced off upstairs again, back to her "madhouse."

On the evening before the show, there was a sort of dress rehearsal, for the benefit of all who worked in the firm. And, for the first time, Marianne fully realized the genius of Florian.

Until then, she had supposed she knew quite a lot about beautiful clothes—the charm, the elegance, the variety which they could encompass. But as the incredible pageant unfolded itself before her dazzled gaze, she experienced a feeling of something like awe. All this— the whole show, the immense business enterprise, the entire structure of an industry that employed hundreds of people—sprang from the inspiration and genius of one man.

She turned her head to look at Florian, who stood at the side of the salon, pale with strain and fatigue, but with an expression of almost boyish eagerness and interest on his face. Almost, thought Marianne, as though he were seeing this all for the first time.

Beside him was a fair-haired, beautiful girl in the loveliest mink coat Marianne had ever seen. And, even as she wondered curiously who the stranger was, Marcelle informed her in a whisper that this was Madame Florian.

"How lovely—and how young!" exclaimed Marianne.

"Not *so* young," Marcelle, to whom thirty seemed a trifle passé. "She was herself a model here, you know. Monsieur Florian took her on, unknown and at the last minute, some years ago, because his star model broke her leg just before the show. Gabrielle, as they called Madame Florian then, had exactly the same coloring and measurements. She even wore the wedding dress. It was an immense sensation. Then he married her."

"What a romantic story," Marianne said, and glanced again at the girl.

"Yes, it was romantic," agreed Marcelle in her solemn way. And then they both fell silent as Lisette glided forth in a breathtaking evening gown, in which layers and layers of gossamerlike chiffon combined the exact shades of her red hair and her green eyes. Against the dress and her shining hair, her skin looked pearly white, and she herself looked faintly unreal.

Silence fell over the room as she went by—only to be succeeded by rapturous exclamations and applause when she had passed. It was the most extraordinary thing. She looked like someone out of a legend, Marianne thought, and she moved like some enchantress casting a spell.

There were many other wonderful dresses and coats and suits that evening. But to Marianne, the almost dangerously arresting moment remained that one when Lisette passed in the green and red dress.

Afterward, to her surprise, Florian himself addressed her in quite a friendly tone.

"Well, *mademoiselle*, how did you enjoy your first fashion show?"

"It was fantastic! I have been telling myself all evening that this comes from the inspiration of one man— and still I can't believe it," Marianne said candidly. "I'm happier than ever, *monsieur*, to be allowed to work here."

"Come, that's a very pretty speech, on the spur of the moment." He gave her that half cynical, half kindly smile. "I hear Madame Rachel is pleased with you."

"I'm very glad, *monsieur*." Marianne smiled and flushed slightly.

"I, too," he said dryly. "In the next few weeks there will be no time to make allowances for inefficiency." Then, as the fair-haired girl came up, he added, "Have

you met my wife? She also is English. Gabrielle, this is
Mademoiselle Marianne, who has come to work in the
boutique.''

"Why, of course! Roger Senloe told me he met you
somewhere. In the boutique itself, wasn't it?'' Gabrielle
Florian took Marianne's hand in a warm and friendly
clasp. "He said he was sure you were going to be a great
success.''

"Did he really?'' Marianne was surprised and gratified. "How nice of him.''

"Particularly as he knows nothing whatever about
the working of the boutique,'' commented Florian, but
not really unkindly. "Come, *chérie*—'' he took his wife
by the arm "—it has been a long enough evening.''

They both bade Marianne good-night. And making
her way through the slowly dispersing crowd of
workers, models, *vendeuses* and others, Marianne went
downstairs again. Here Madame Rachel waited to give
the absolutely final instructions for the morrow. But she
was cool and calm, like a good general before battle.

"And now—'' she addressed her staff collectively
"—you must go home and sleep well. For tomorrow
you will need all your strength and energy.''

Tingling already with a sort of anticipatory excitement, Marianne said good-night and went out into the
street, telling herself that this had been one of the really
memorable evenings of her life.

The cold air struck sharply on her cheeks, and she
gave a slight gasp. But not only because of the cold. For
there, in the light that streamed from the windows of the
boutique, stood Nat, with a welcoming smile on his
dark, attractive face.

"Nat!'' She ran to him, with all the pent-up eagerness
of weeks in her voice. "How won—''

And then she stopped. For his expression changed to
astonishment, and then to something like perplexity,
and in a horrible moment of realization she knew that
the welcoming smile had not been for her. He had been
looking past her—and now she turned her head and
looked, too.

For the second time that evening she caught her breath in a gasp. For Lisette was standing in the doorway, not half a dozen yards from her—her full red mouth drawn into a sullen line and her green eyes narrowed to almost catlike slits.

CHAPTER THREE

IT WAS AN appalling moment for Marianne as she stood there, feeling that she was nothing but an unwelcome barrier between Nat and Lisette. But then, with a composure that astonished herself, she forced both voice and expression into some semblance of naturalness.

"Why, Nat—" she said, and this time her tone was that of any girl greeting any pleasant acquaintance unexpectedly, "I thought for a moment you'd found out where I worked. But I see you've come to fetch Lisette. I mustn't keep you."

"But—wait a moment!" Nat, too, had now recovered himself, and he caught her by the hand, with an eagerness that made her feel a little better. "I had no idea you were working here. Lisette didn't tell me."

"Lisette didn't even know you and I knew each other. How could she?" And, with a smile that cost her a good deal, Marianne turned, as though to include Lisette in this conversation.

The other girl approached slowly, and although her face no longer wore that extraordinarily dangerous expression, she still looked very much on the defensive, as though she thought she might at any moment find it necessary to assert herself in no uncertain manner.

"Mr. Gilmore is an old friend of mine, Lisette," Marianne said. "You must forgive me if I assumed he had come here to meet me."

"He has come to meet *me*," stated Lisette unequivocally, determined evidently that this at least should be clear, whatever else might be obscure about the situation.

"So I see." Marianne's tone was colder than she had

intended. "We must see each other another time, Nat. I—"

"But wait a minute!" he exclaimed again, and his hand tightened on hers. "I don't want to lose you now I've found you again. Where can I get hold of you?"

"Why, you know, surely? Didn't they give you my address at home?"

"Only the first one. Then your mother said you'd moved, and that she would tell me when she got the new one. But she never did because—oh, quite a lot has happened, Marianne. I haven't seen anything of the family for some while—"

"I know. Yvonne wrote and told me. Don't worry, Nat. I completely understand. But if you had written to my first Paris address they would have sent it on. I left word—"

"Yes, I daresay. But—" he hesitated, looked put out, and then smiled at her, the old engaging, sparkling smile she remembered with such heartwarming joy "—I guess I've been rather silly about this. Though—"

"Are we going somewhere to eat, or shall I go home?" inquired Lisette at this moment, and her tone implied that she had heard just about as much of the joint affairs of Marianne and Nat as she cared to take.

"I'm sorry!" Nat laughed and took her by the arm, with an easy intimacy that made Marianne wince. "I mustn't keep you hanging about any longer, Lisette. But Marianne and I are old friends and—"

"This I have already been told, and it is not especially interesting to me," Lisette pointed out a trifle sulkily.

"Then we'll go." Nat gave Marianne a quick smile, which seemed to invite her to share his amused indulgence toward Lisette—an invitation she felt unable to accept. "Here's my phone number—" He scribbled on a page torn from his diary and handed it to her. "Give me a call, and we'll go out somewhere together and catch up on each other's news."

"That will be fine," Marianne said. Then she bade the other two goodbye and turned away.

But it was not fine at all, of course. She simply hated

the idea of leaving Nat to go with Lisette, while she—the onlooker once more, the understanding friend—took herself off home alone.

Don't be unreasonable, she admonished herself, as she walked along the brightly lit Paris streets. *What else could he do? He'd already invited her out. He could hardly leave her flat. And still less could he take us both.* And she actually laughed a little at the thought of such a gruesome trio.

At least I know where to find him now. And I know—more or less—why he didn't get in touch with me before. That nice Roger Senloe was right—her heart warmed a little to the absent Roger Senloe at this thought—*Nat felt a bit self-conscious toward me because I am Yvonne's sister. He would have looked me up all right if it had been easy and straightforward. But with the broken engagement complicating everything, he couldn't bring himself to make a special effort.*

This reflection soothed her anxious feelings immensely. She was able to tell herself that now everything would be different. She and Nat would meet constantly, with no barrier between them. Lisette was no more than a minor incident in his life. He *couldn't* really take anyone of her caliber seriously.

Or could he? For a moment, Marianne remembered uneasily the indulgent glance he had given when Lisette had chosen to pout and look sulky. On anyone but Nat she would have characterized it as a fatuous glance.

But I'm prejudiced, she thought. *I'm not being cool and objective.*

Then she remembered Roger Senloe saying that it was extraordinarily difficult to be objective and levelheaded where one's deepest feelings were concerned. How right he was! He was really a very penetrating person—besides being so nice.

Perhaps as a relief from more anxious speculation, she allowed her thoughts to linger pleasantly on Roger Senloe. It pleased her to think he had spoken so well of her to Madame Florian. And still more that he had evidently made no mention of the real circumstances in which they had met. Even though he and Gabrielle Florian were presumably on very good terms.

How good, Marianne wondered idly. How did one feel toward a very nice man one had nearly married? And again she could not help thinking that in Gabrielle's place she would have chosen the Englishman rather than the Frenchman.

He'd make a much easier sort of husband, thought Marianne with a smile.

But Florian, of course, had the unique fascination of genius. And what genius! Her mind was back again now at the rehearsal of the fashion show that she had seen that evening, and that prompted a fresh sensation of excited anticipation of tomorrow's opening day.

It would be wrong to say that these reflections ousted Nat from her mind. He was there, in the back of her consciousness, during her sleeping as well as her waking hours. But when Marianne woke to a cold, brilliant February morning, in her room high under the eaves, she knew this was going to be a day she would remember for the rest of her life.

She bathed, dressed and breakfasted quickly. And then, exquisitely trim from her smooth, shining hair to the tips of her admirably cut shoes, she ran downstairs. On the way she was overtaken by Sadie Farrell, a gay young American student who knew about her job at the Florian boutique.

"My, how I envy you today!" she exclaimed. "Here am I going off to moldy old lectures on medieval French poetry, while you're going to watch *the* fashion show of the year and see all sorts of famous people into the bargain."

"I shan't see much of the fashion show itself," Marianne assured her, smiling. "I'll be downstairs in the boutique."

"But you'll see all the celebrities going up there?"

"Yes, I expect so. And I saw the show last night."

"You did?" If Marianne had claimed to see Solomon in all his glory Sadie could not have looked more impressed. "What is it like?"

"Marvelous," said Marianne, enthusiastically but uninformatively.

"All frightfully secret, of course?"

"Oh, yes. No questions answered until after today," Marianne agreed with a laugh. "Today is the big opening show, of course. Then tomorrow comes the press show in the morning, and in the afternoon there is the show for the big international buyers."

"And what do you do in all that?" Sadie wanted to know.

"Stay downstairs in the boutique, respectfully wafting the distinguished guests up the stairs, lightly spraying them with our new and heavenly perfume, and generally making them feel that the whole thing has just been put on for their special benefit. Then we have to be ready to show and discuss our new stock if they want to see this on their way down again."

"It sounds heaven to me. Why am I still at university?" groaned Sadie. "What's particularly lovely in the boutique this season, Marianne?"

"Everything," declared Marianne, promptly and loyally. "But best of all is the costume jewelry, I think. I've never seen such beautiful stuff."

"I'll have to come in and see it, even if I can't afford to buy any," Sadie said.

"Do. But we're also having a terrific display of it at the Charities Spring Fair in a couple of weeks' time. It's going to be a splendid affair, from what I hear. A lot of topgrade stuff will be on show, quite apart from what is for sale."

"And will you be in charge?"

"Not in charge, exactly. But I hope to be there. It's in the evening, you know, at the Opéra. A gala performance in the theater itself and a sort of luxury trade display in the Hall of Mirrors."

"Oh, Marianne! I suppose it's going to cost the earth and a half to get in?"

"To the gala performance—yes, I suppose so. But I don't know about the fair itself. I'll see what I can do," Marianne promised. And then she had to bid Sadie a hurried goodbye and to go on her way, for it would never do to be late on this day, of all days.

When she arrived at Florian's, excitement was already running fever-high, and Célestine—who had been upstairs on some errand for Madame Rachel—reported that tears were already flowing in the models' dressing room. Two of the girls had even been understood to say that they felt too overwrought to go on.

"They will get over it," declared Madame Rachel, unmoved. "It is always like this. It makes them feel sensitive and important."

"But doesn't it drive poor Monsieur Florian nearly mad with worry?" inquired Marianne sympathetically.

"No, no. Madame Moisant would never let him hear of a little thing like that," Madame Rachel assured her. "Only if one of the girls were to throw herself out of the window would she mention the matter. And this would not happen."

"Then it's Madame Moisant who does the worrying?" suggested Marianne curiously.

The other lady shrugged.

"She is well paid for this worry," Madame Rachel stated significantly. "And anyway, she knows quite well that the moment the girls have to go out and face their public, all will be smiles and tranquillity. Not one of them would be so silly as to spoil her makeup with real tears after a certain moment in proceedings. Even pique and envy take second place to vanity and self-interest."

Marianne gave a slightly shocked laugh.

"It sounds terrifying," she remarked.

"It is merely part of the day," returned Madame Rachel calmly. "Nevertheless," she added a trifle smugly, "it is better to be down here, where all is sane and tranquil."

"Sane" and "tranquil" were not quite the words Marianne would have used to describe the boutique on this particular morning. For, though infinitely elegant, it was rather small and, with everyone moving about on some last-minute task or other, it seemed to be buzzing with activity.

However, at last no one showed signs of breaking into tears. And when at last the first guests began to arrive for the great fashion show, Madame Rachel, with her minions in attendance, received and wafted onward these fortunate creatures, in the manner of a queen detailing her ladies of honor for social duties on an occasion of international importance.

In this way, Marianne found herself personally conducting one of France's most famous actresses up the thickly carpeted stairs, to deliver her almost literally into the outstretched hands of Madame Moisant.

It was all very emotional and exciting. Something between prize day at school and presentation day at court, Marianne could not help thinking. And over it all hung the smiling suspense usually associated only with the opening night of a much discussed play.

Now people were coming thick and fast, and Marianne had just returned downstairs for the fourth time when a familiar voice at her side said, "Hello. How are you enjoying the world of haute couture?"

"Oh, Mr. Senloe—" she turned eagerly to greet him "—how nice! I didn't know you came to the opening show."

"I don't usually. It's not really up my alley. But I promised Gabrielle I'd come this time. She vows it's going to be Florian's biggest success yet."

"I shouldn't wonder. I thought the rehearsal marvelous last night."

"And you're enjoying life here?" He stood looking down at her, his gray eyes kindly.

"Oh, yes, indeed!"

"And—the other matter? Did it straighten out all right?" He sounded genuinely interested, rather than curious.

"The other—? Oh, well, I think it will. You were quite right—" she dropped her voice and spoke rapidly "—he did feel self-conscious because of his broken engagement. That was why he hadn't looked me up. But we met by chance last night—"

"Only last night?" His eyebrows went up.

"Yes, but—it was all right then. He explained, and we arranged to meet soon. I think it's going to be all right again."

"I'm so glad." He smiled. "But I mustn't keep you. I'm sure you're greatly in demand."

"It's all right, really. We're supposed to be welcoming all of the guests."

"But not to concentrate on one." He laughed. "I know the drill, you see. Well, I'll look out for you later, if you're not too busy."

And with a friendly little nod he went on up the stairs, while Marianne turned, in obedience to a tap on her arm from Madame Rachel, to attend to another distinguished visitor.

Chatter and laughter, greetings and exclamation now filled the salon and spilled down the stairs, to meet further waves of similar sound and excitement coming up from the boutique. Everyone seemed in high good humor. Though, according to Madame Rachel, who had given Marianne some worldly comments beforehand, much of this seeming good humor covered a great deal of professional envy and malice.

Finally the hour for the opening struck, and comparative silence fell on the assembly upstairs. Everyone but the latest of latecomers had now arrived. Every inch of the salon and the passage leading from it to the head of the stairs was crammed. Far away, Marianne heard the penetrating tones of Madame Moisant, and although she could not distinguish the words, she knew that the first model was being announced.

Something between a rustle and a sigh passed over the company. The show had begun.

So long as they kept a watchful eye on the boutique, the girls were allowed to stand on the stairs to catch a glimpse of each model as she paraded not only through the salon, but along the passage as far as the head of the stairs before turning back to the dressing room.

Even to be on the fringe of the great show was something. And the extraordinary thing was that, without words or any clearly definable means, the subtle awareness of yet another Florian triumph began to drift through the rooms and to permeate even to the boutique.

It was not only the frequent applause heard from afar, though there was plenty of that. It was not even the occasional exclamation or comment that one heard from the people seated nearest to the head of the stairs. It was something quite intangible, but also quite unmistakable.

"I begin to smell the perfume of success," remarked Madame Rachel with a knowledgeable little movement of her head. And Marianne thought she knew what was meant.

The show ended in a storm of applause for the superb wedding dress. And then it seemed that suddenly everyone was released from a sort of spell. Chairs were pushed back, talking broke out afresh. There was a good deal of kissing and gushing. "Especially from those who were green with envy," as Madame Rachel said. And then down the stairs streamed the guests once more—those who were not lingering to discuss future sales—and the boutique was filled with eager inquirers and admirers.

For the rest of the day Marianne had not a moment to herself. All was activity, gaiety, congratulation and a great deal of business. She caught sight of Roger Senloe once more, but only from a distance, and she was not able to exchange more than a smile with him over the heads of eager customers. However, he made a significant upward movement of his thumb, to indicate that he thought the show a success, and she nodded in agreement.

There was a ceaseless stream and counterstream of customers and staff, the incessant ringing of telephones, the coming and going of photographers. Then from time to time one or other of the models would come down, clad in photogenic glory, to be posed and photographed on the steps of the famous fashion house.

On more than one occasion Lisette made her appearance. And finally she came down wearing the breathtaking red and green evening dress.

"It is to be in color," she informed Marianne, who happened to be within speaking range while Lisette stood waiting for the photographers to prime their cameras and arrange their lights. "I am glad. It is for the cover on one of the leading magazines. Now Nat will really see me as I would wish—on every paper stall in Paris."

"How nice," said Marianne. But she knew from Lisette's small, secret smile that she had not sounded at all as though she thought it nice. How could she?

"We went to the Polichinelle last night," Lisette went on, gratuitously. "It is our favorite restaurant."

"Really?" Marianne's tone was cold and lifeless, and she turned away as though only interested in a customer who was examining some of the wonderful evening scarves, which had been drawing exclamation of delight and admiration all day.

"It was there," went on Lisette's voice behind her, "that Nat first told me he loved me."

Marianne turned as though she had been shot, and stared at the other girl.

"He told you—Nat told you—that?"

"Most certainly." Lisette smoothed a fold of her glorious skirt with meticulous care. "This is something I would have you remember very particularly if you should meet him."

And, still smiling to herself in that secret way, she went out to the photographers, who were now calling impatiently for her.

Marianne stood stock-still, even the customers forgotten for some blank and horrible moments. Nat—loved—that girl. Or thought he did, which was just as bad. Particularly as he had not kept his thoughts to himself, but had clothed them in indiscreet words.

It was there—at the Secret de Polichinelle—that he had told Lisette he loved her. Perhaps on that very evening when Marianne had seen them there.

Oh, why had she fled from the scene, on that ridiculous impulse of panic and humiliation? Why had she not walked up boldly to Nat and spoken to him? Perhaps

she might have saved him from what she could only
regard as a disastrous step. Nat—and Lisette! It was not
to be thought of! Not after all she had gone through on
Yvonne's account.

"Marianne!" Madame Rachel spoke in a sibilant
whisper, which carried, however, a great deal of
authority. "You are forgetting your work. This is not
the day or the place for dreaming."

It certainly was not. And, with a jerk that almost
hurt, Marianne recalled herself to the immediate present.

"I'm sorry, *madame*. I wasn't thinking—"

"I know." Madame Rachel's tone was more sympathetic. "Suddenly one feels blank. But one must smile
and be active, just the same."

So Marianne somehow smiled and became "active"
once more, and presumably she managed quite well, for
there were no more reproofs from Madame Rachel.
Only at the back of her mind all the time were those
words of Lisette—"It was there that Nat first told me he
loved me."

Not until a good hour after their usual closing time
did Madame Rachel announce that it was time to shut
the doors of the boutique on one of the most successful
days they had ever had. And even then, activity upstairs
seemed undiminished.

There was still a good deal of clearing up to be done,
and presently Madame Rachel gave Marianne a sheaf of
papers and told her to take them to Monsieur Florian's
office.

"You will give them to him personally if he is there. If
not, you will find him—or wait until he comes. These
are the returns of sale for the day. And they are," added
Madame Rachel complacently, "sensational."

"Oh, *madame*, don't you want to give them to him
yourself, and have the credit?" Marianne smiled at her.

But Madame Rachel shook her head.

"*Pas du tout!* He will want to discuss them. I know
Monsieur Florian on opening day. He is like a child with
a toy. He cannot hear enough or say enough about the

new success. And me—I am dying on my feet. I prefer to die in my bed." And she smiled cheerfully, looking very much alive—but certainly a little exhausted at
last.

So Marianne climbed the stairs for the hundredth
time that day, realizing suddenly that her legs and back
and head were aching, and went along to Monsieur
Florian's office.

She was lucky enough to find him there, and she knew
immediately from the almost feverish glitter in his eyes
that he was a very well-satisfied man, even though he
was pale and worn with the strain of that day and a
good many crowded yesterdays.

"Madame Rachel asked me to bring you these returns, *monsieur*." Marianne laid them on the desk.

"So?" He took them and ran a comprehensive glance
over them. "Sit down, *mademoiselle*," he said, without
looking up. "Today is not a day to stand, unless one is
forced to do so."

Marianne sank thankfully into a chair, reflecting as
she did so that it was not quite true what they said of
Monsieur Florian in the firm—that, so long as his affairs went well, he wouldn't notice if you were dying until he heard the thump as you hit the floor.

"Phe-no-men-al!" she heard him murmur, with a
satisfied pause between each syllable. Then he looked
up and said with almost boyish enjoyment, "It was an
exciting day, eh, *mademoiselle*?"

"Tremendously exciting, *monsieur*."

"What did you like best in the collection?"

"I, *monsieur*?" Marianne smiled, somehow touched
as well as amused that even her opinion could be of
interest to him. "I thought," she said slowly, "that the
most remarkable dress was the red and green evening
dress that Lisette wore."

"Number sixty-three? But you did not actually like
it." His tone made that a statement rather than a question. "Why not?"

"I—I did like it, *monsieur*. At least—"

"It is a frightening dress on Lisette," he observed

calmly. "But it also fascinates one. I am interested that you feel it so strongly."

"It's partly—Lisette herself," Marianne could not help saying.

"Yes, of course. Lisette is a rather frightening young woman. I should not wish a good friend of mine to marry Lisette, shall we say? But—" He stopped suddenly and fixed Marianne with that cool, thoughtful glance of his. "What disturbs you about that, *petite*?" His faintly cynical tone altered suddenly.

"N—nothing, *monsieur*." Marianne stared back at him with widened gaze, wishing that she could add something casual and amusing, but knowing well that all her anxiety was in her eyes.

"I—see," he said thoughtfully. And Marianne immediately had the absurd and incredible conviction that he did see. Almost everything to do with herself—and Nat—and Lisette. "So you and Lisette are in some way rivals?"

"Oh, no!"

Then suddenly he smiled, and for an odd moment she thought she glimpsed why Madame Florian had married him.

"Shall I tell you something, *chérie*, for your peace of mind?" he said, and although there was an amused glint in his eyes, it was not unkindly. "Our good friends seldom marry the Lisettes of this world."

"Perhaps it is enough if they love them, *monsieur*," retorted Marianne, before she could stop herself.

"And he loves her?" Florian shook his head skeptically.

"S—so he says."

"Did he say so to you?"

"Oh, no. To her. She told me so herself—this afternoon."

"*She* told you? Zut!" Florian laughed contemptuously. "She finds it difficult to tell the truth even if it suits her, that one. She would not think of telling it if a lie would suit her better. Pay no attention to her, *petite*. I would want something more than the unsupported word of Lisette before I would lose sleep over any statement of hers.''

"Oh, Monsieur Florian—'' Marianne smiled faintly in spite of herself ''—do you really mean that?''

"Of course.'' Having pronounced on the matter, he as good as dismissed it with a flick of his well-shaped hand. Then he looked back at the papers before him, and Marianne had the impression that her audience was over.

"Th-thank you, *monsieur*.'' She got to her feet. "I can't imagine why I told you so much—''

"You couldn't help it,'' he said simply, and she wondered quite what he meant by that.

"But, please—you won't mention anything about this to anyone, will you?''

"I never mention confidences to anyone, *mademoiselle*.'' He gave her a dry glance. "There is enough gossip and scandal in this place without my contributing to it. Now go home, there's a good child, and have a good night's rest. If today is any indication of the business we shall do in the next few weeks, you need all the rest you can get.''

She actually laughed at that, and found suddenly that she felt immeasurably cheered. She bade her employer an almost cheerful good-night, and then went away—as many other people had gone from that office before—with the curious conviction that if Monsieur Florian said a thing was so, then it was so.

I don't believe there's anything between Nat and Lisette, she told herself determinedly as she ran downstairs. *I believe everything is going to be all right. I have only to call him. He gave me the number himself—*

And then, as though in almost uncanny confirmation of her thoughts, Marcelle said, as she arrived in the boutique once more, "Someone telephoned for you. An Englishman, with a nice speaking voice.''

"An Englishman?''

"Yes. He left a number for you to call back. I scribbed it on the pad there.''

"I have his number. Oh, no—perhaps this is his office—''

Anyway, it didn't matter. Whatever the number, Nat was at the other end—waiting for her.

She could have laughed aloud now at the absurd and sulky threats of Lisette. How fortunate that Monsieur Florian had made that intuitive guess—and then reassured her. Marianne found it difficult not to chatter her happy thoughts aloud as she dialed the number with slightly unsteady fingers.

And she stood there, listening to the ringing tone, it seemed to her that her heart beat in answering rhythm.

Than a pleasant voice said in her ear, "Hello. This is Roger Senloe speaking."

CHAPTER FOUR

"R-ROGER SENLOE?" repeated Marianne, so blankly that her reaction must have carried even over the telephone wires.

"Well—yes. Is it such a blow?" He laughed, but she could hear he was rather put out.

"No—no, of course not." She tried to collect her thoughts, to bring them back from Nat and concentrate them on Roger Senloe. "I'm sorry. I was just—surprised. I—I was expecting someone else to ring, and I thought—it was he."

"I'm sorry to be the wrong one." There was still that mixture of amusement and chagrin in his voice.

"Oh, no—really, you mustn't say that. And please forgive my rudeness." Now she was in better command of herself. "I'm just a bit dazed after the busiest day I've ever known, and I don't think I quite know what I'm saying."

"I daresay not." His tone was sympathetic now. "That was really why I called. I know what these opening days are like and how flat out everyone is by the end. I wondered if you would like me to take you out for a quiet meal somewhere, or if you just want to go home to bed."

A quiet meal—with someone else doing all the ordering and arranging! Suddenly Marianne realized she had had little to eat all day and that she was ravenous.

"Oh, that sounds simply heavenly! I'm not at my scintillating best, but if you really mean it—"

"Of course I do. Unless the other chap—the right one—" she could not really resent the note of amusement in his voice "—intended to take you."

"No. At least, we hadn't made any arrangement."

Rapidly she decided that she would telephone Nat another evening. Tomorrow evening—or, at any rate, sometime when she felt less exhausted and more able to deal with a problematic situation.

"I should love to come," she told Roger Senloe firmly. "Where shall I meet you?"

"I'll fetch you in my car in ten minutes' time, if that's all right."

With difficulty she kept herself from saying that nothing could be more all right, and she replaced the receiver, with the odd feeling that this was the only bearable ending to a thrilling but wearing day.

Nice, undemanding Roger Senloe! She didn't have to pretend with him, or keep her feelings under strict and anxious control. She didn't have to wonder distractedly if he were in love with Lisette, or if there were some subtle way in which she could find out the real truth. She could just relax, metaphorically sit back and let him do any worrying there might be.

"You're going out this evening?" Marcelle watched solemnly as Marianne added a rapid touch of makeup to her pale face. "I don't know how you have the energy."

"*I* wouldn't have known five minutes ago," Marianne admitted with a laugh. "But sometimes it's easier to go out, and let someone else do the arranging, than to try to work things out for oneself. With the right kind of man—"

"Ah, yes—with the right man all is different," agreed Marcelle, her face lighting up unexpectedly. Then she added, with almost naive curiosity, "Are you very much in love with him?"

"Not in the least," said Marianne heartily. "That's why I'm going with him."

"I do not understand," Marcelle began gravely. But at that moment the telephone rang again, and as Marianne and she were now the only people left in the boutique, Marcelle said obligingly, "I will answer it, while you finish getting ready."

But hardly had she taken up the receiver before she observed, "It is for you. Your beau back again."

"Oh. . . ." Feeling suddenly that she could not bear to be done out of her pleasant relaxation now, Marianne hurried over to the telephone. "Hello, Roger! Is anything—"

"Roger nothing," a familiar voice replied. "This is Nat speaking."

"*Nat*!" Her whole being glowed with rapture and delight. "How wonderful! You only just caught me. I was putting on my hat."

"Well, I knew you'd be late. Lisette told me it would be a long day for all of you today. But I thought I'd chance it now."

"Yes—of course." The mention of Lisette served to cool her eagerness slightly. "It's been a wonderful day. But a killer, too. We've only just closed the boutique, and some of the girls are still working upstairs."

"Lisette seemed to think she might be there until midnight," Nat agreed. "I wondered if you and I could make a date of it this evening."

Because Lisette was unavailable, Marianne wondered uneasily. And then she dismissed the thought as unworthy.

"Nat, I'm sorry. I've already arranged to go out to supper with someone else."

"Have you really?" He sounded disappointed. "With Roger, I presume?"

"Yes. How did you know? Oh, of course, I greeted you as Roger, didn't I?"

"You did. And spoiled my evening." He laughed, but he also sounded as though his evening were really spoiled.

"I'm terribly sorry," she said again. "I wish I'd known beforehand."

"You mean you'd have ditched Roger for me, if there'd still been time?"

"Certainly not! I'm not that sort of girl. I mean I wouldn't have accepted his invitation, which was given only five minutes ago."

"Only five minutes ago!" Nat sounded really vexed. "Can't you get out of it?"

"No, of course not. But let's make another date, Nat. How about tomorrow evening?"

But Nat didn't seem to know how free he would be on the following evening.

"Then some other evening in the week when you do know you'll be free."

"It's a bit difficult—"

She had a sudden and almost savage impulse to say angrily, "Lisette will be working late every evening this week, if that's what's troubling you!" But somehow she refrained.

And, at that moment Marcelle made a signal to her and said quietly. "Your friend with the car is outside."

"Nat, I must go—I'm sorry. Roger has arrived to collect me. But I'll call you. Or you call me. But not here during the daytime."

"You *are* hedged around with restrictions, aren't you?" he said crossly.

"No more than Lisette is," she returned a little curtly. And then she hung up.

She was ashamed of herself, as soon as she had done that. And she was annoyed to have shown she *was* annoyed. But there is always a point at which control snaps, and very seldom is it at the wisest point.

Marianne turned to find Marcelle regarding her with solemn interest. Marcelle regarded most things and people with solemn interest.

"*He* is the man you love," she observed with conviction. "Why do you not go out with him?"

"Because I've already promised to go out with someone else," replied Marianne impatiently. "Besides—" she hesitated aware that she actually preferred to go with Roger Senloe at this moment "—the other one is so nice and restful and won't ask me awkward questions or make me wonder what he means," she said, in a sudden burst of confidence.

"These are good qualities to live with," Marcelle agreed seriously. "It is strange how seldom one loves them."

"But one can like them immensely," Marianne countered. "Good night, Marcelle. Thank you for doing the final clearing. You're a good, kind colleague."

"Also I have no beau at the moment," replied Marcelle with a slight sigh. "That leaves one free for other things."

"Oh, darling, we'll find you a wonderful beau!" exclaimed Marianne, deciding that Roger must wait just three minutes longer while she reassured Marcelle. "You have such beautiful eyes and such kind, gentle ways—it won't be difficult. And then *I'll* do the clearing up, while you go out to meet him."

Marcelle laughed unexpectedly at this, and looked so truly pretty as she flushed that Marianne thought, *I don't believe anyone's ever called her "darling" before, or told her she has beautiful eyes—which she has.*

Aloud, she asked curiously, "Marcelle, do you live on your own?"

"No. I live with my *maman*, who is something of an invalid. She is very patient and does not ask much, so long as I am at home with her in the evenings."

"O-oh," said Marianne, not much liking the sound of this patient *maman*. "Well, one can always rearrange things, if one is determined. We'll see. Good night, Marcelle—and thank you for everything."

And, gathering up her bag and gloves, she ran out to the waiting car.

"I'm so sorry! I was delayed for a few minutes and—"

"Don't apologize," Roger Senloe told her. "Just sit back and relax. Do you want to go anywhere special?"

"You choose," Marianne begged him. "So long as it's fairly quiet and no one there wants me to show them bags, scarves, gloves or costume jewelery, it will do for me."

He laughed and said, "Leave it to me." So she willingly did, and presently she found herself sitting opposite him at a corner table in a quiet, homely little restaurant in the less fashionable part of the city, with the most delicious *sole bonne femme* she had ever tasted before her.

"Oh, Mr. Senloe, how do you *find* these places?" she asked with a contented sigh.

"By looking for them with great diligence, in a city I love and know very well," he assured her with a smile.

"And how did you know exactly what it was that I needed, at the end of this glorious but most exacting day?"

He looked across at her and his eyes twinkled.

"I practiced quite a lot on Gabrielle Florian, don't forget."

"Oh, yes—of course!"

"There wasn't much I didn't know about fashion house nerves by the time she married him," he declared, with a wry smile.

"What a shame—" Marianne began. And then, before she could stop herself, "You know, I can't imagine why she married Florian rather than you."

"Thank you for those kind words." He grinned. "I've sometimes wondered myself."

"Was it long ago?"

"It depends what you mean by 'long.' It's just five years ago tonight since Gabrielle came out with me for the first time, after making a sensation at Florian's fashion show as a completely unknown model."

"You don't say!" Marianne glanced at him curiously and wondered for a moment if she were taking part in some sort of nostalgic reconstruction for him.

"And the odd thing is that she, too, really wanted to go out with someone else."

"With Monsieur Florian?"

"Oh, no! He was just her alarming employer at that point. With some fellow she'd once been engaged to. I've forgotten his name now, and I expect she had, too. He just didn't count later."

"I see. But there's one thing I must put right. I *didn't* want to go out with someone else. I merely mistook you for someone else on the phone."

"Sure?" He smiled at her.

"Quite sure. As a matter of fact, he called up five minutes after you and wanted me to go out with him.

And although I wouldn't have done so anyway, of course, after arranging to go with you, it did make me realize that I actually preferred to go with someone kind and unproblematic like you.''

"How very nice of you. I suppose some men would rather be regarded as problematic devils than soothing supports. I've never been able to decide myself which I would really prefer.''

"I don't think one could make a devil out of you, in any case,'' Marianne said, regarding him reflectively. "And tonight at any rate I'm profoundly glad of that.''

They both laughed then, and began to talk with an added degree of intimacy. And presently they were calling each other Marianne and Roger, and she had told him quite a lot about her family, and he had explained that, as the only son of a minor ambassador, he had inevitably gravitated toward the diplomatic service—a life that on the whole, he greatly enjoyed.

But even though they chatted enthusiastically, he kept a watchful eye on the time, and firmly took her home before she could begin to feel weary again.

"I have to go to Geneva for a few days,'' he told her, as they bade each other good-night. "But when I come back we must do this again.''

She said truly that nothing would please her more. And then they parted, and she climbed the long stairs to her room, wondering a little as she did so if he had gone back to his apartment to dream nostalgically of that evening five years ago.

THE NEXT DAY, if not as hectic as the opening day, was very busy indeed, and Marianne had little time to ponder her own affairs. But the thought of Nat—and the curt way she had parted from him—hovered uneasily in the background of her mind all day. And when she finally reached home that evening, she telephoned to him, even though he had been humiliatingly vague about the time he might have available.

His voice answered her immediately, and she was so relieved that she broke into quick, eager explanation.

"Oh, Nat—it's Marianne. I'm sorry I cut you off so abruptly last night, but I was getting nervous, keeping Roger waiting, and—"

"Is he such a tyrant, then?"

"No, of course not. Don't be silly! Only—well, never mind. When am I going to see you, Nat? It seems such ages since we had a really good talk."

"It *is* ages," he assured her. "Much too long." And all at once his voice took on all the old warmth and interest. "What about this evening, Marianne? Are you free?"

"Yes, I'm free. But I thought you—"

"That's all right. What I was expecting didn't turn up. Why don't we drive out along the river? I know a nice little place, about an hour's drive out, that doesn't depend too much on fine summer weather for its charm. How about it?"

"It sounds ideal to me."

"Then meet me outside the Opéra in half an hour. I'll be driving a small red—but what am I talking about? You know the old bus, of course."

"Oh, Nat, have you got your own car here with you? How nice. It will be like old times."

"Not too much like old times," he growled, and she remembered Yvonne and felt sorry for him.

"Just enough to make us feel at ease," she said, "and not enough to spoil a new chapter in any way."

"Very nicely said!" He laughed good-humoredly. "In half an hour, then."

It was all going to be perfectly all right! She actually hummed to herself in her happiness as she got ready. And so eager was she not to keep him waiting that she was at the rendezvous ten minutes before time.

He arrived very promptly, however, and was evidently pleased to find her ready waiting.

"Hop in," he instructed her. "I'm not supposed to wait here, and that French cop has the eye of an eagle and the tongue of a macaw."

Obediently Marianne got in, and the car shot away again, threading its way through the traffic in a way that excited both her admiration and her alarm. There was no question of any sustained conversation until they were clear of the center of the city. And then, before she could introduce any subject of her own choosing, he asked almost defiantly, "Were you very shocked about Yvonne and me?"

"No, Nat." With difficulty she prevented herself from saying it had been the greatest moment of her life when she heard the news of their broken engagement. "I'm truly sorry if either of you felt deeply hurt. But I was never very happy about that engagement."

"Weren't you really?" He turned his head for a moment and looked at her. "Why not?"

"I thought she left you too often on your own for her to be really in love with you. And I couldn't see you as the husband of someone who put her work first."

"Then you don't blame me?"

"No, Nat—of course not! People must settle these things for themselves. If you and Yvonne decided you couldn't make a go of it, I can't see that it's the business of anyone but yourselves. Particularly as neither of you treated the other badly."

"I'm glad you feel like that." He gave something like a sigh of relief, and for a moment he took one hand off the wheel of the car and patted her hand affectionately.

"Oh, Nat! Did you worry about my attitude?"

"A bit—yes. You and I have always been such good friends—you've always been the most wonderful confidante and safety valve. I couldn't bear the idea that all that was over."

"There was no question of our friendship being over," said Marianne, trying to decide if it were a compliment or not, to be regarded as a wonderful confidante and safety valve. "Was that why you didn't make it your business to find me in Paris?"

"I suppose so." He smiled rather remorsefully. "Too stupid to mope around without doing anything about it, wasn't it?"

"It was rather," she agreed sympathetically. But then she remembered Lisette. And something stronger than herself made her say, "But you did find *some* compensation, didn't you?"

"Did I?" He looked surprised. "What do you mean?"

"How about the charming little redhead at Florian's?

To her incredulous astonishment, she actually managed to make that sound light and amused.

"Oh—Lisette!" He laughed. "She is charming, isn't she?"

"Very," said Marianne coldly.

"You mean you don't like her?"

"I don't really know her well. I suppose she's more a man's girl than the kind of girl who tends to be popular with her own sex," Marianne stated, in a tone that she strove to make objective.

"I could imagine that." Nat grinned reflectively, and she clenched her hands to keep herself from demanding why. "She's quite enchanting, in her own way."

"You mean you're—sweet on her?"

"Oh, Marianne, for heaven's sake! I've only just emerged from a broken engagement. You don't surely expect me to start getting entangled with someone else in a matter of weeks?"

"N-no. No, of course not." She bent her head and with difficulty kept herself from bursting into tears of relief. "I just thought—I was a little worried about you. Some men do silly things after—after the kind of experience you've had."

"Such as getting engaged to the next pretty girl they meet?" He looked amused.

"Well—at least they throw around casual assertions that they love someone else, more or less to boost up their own morale, I suppose."

"I'm not that sort of man at all," Nat stated unequivocally. "Now let's leave the subject of broken engagements and talk about ourselves."

So that was what they did. And very delightful it was, too. But nothing else that Nat said to her that evening could compare with the joy of hearing him say, "I'm not that sort of man at all."

It was a lie, then, that assertion of Lisette's. A cool, barefaced, calculated lie. Florian had been quite right. (Was he ever very far wrong? Marianne wondered respectfully.) Lisette had merely employed her own individual technique for warning off a potential rival.

At this moment Marianne could have laughed in her relief and thankfulness. But then she felt a slow indignation rising in her. Lisette just did not deserve to get away with this.

It was impossible, of course, even to Marianne, to tell Nat frankly what Lisette had claimed, richly though she deserved to be shown up. *But I'll speak to her myself,* thought Marianne. *I'll let her know that I know she lied. I don't expect it will cause her any real shame, but at least she shan't go on congratulating herself for having made a monkey of me.*

None of this showed in her manner or expression during the happy evening she spent with Nat. Indeed, most of these reflections came to her only when she was home again and free to think, first how wonderful it was to be in close contact with Nat again, and secondly how nearly Lisette had spoiled everything.

But of these two reflections, only the first one really mattered. And angry though she was with Lisette, she might well have refrained from really putting her resolution into practice if the perfect opportunity had not presented itself the very next day.

One of the more favored press photographers wanted a shot of Lisette in one of the deceptively simple "little" dresses for which Florian was famous, and it was decided to have two or three outstanding articles from the boutique on a table beside her.

Marianne was sent upstairs with a suitable selection—and then there was a long wait, while Florian and the photographer discussed at length some knotty point of display.

Lisette, appealing and yet provocative in her "little" dress, stood quite near Marianne, waiting while the two men arranged, rearranged and discussed. And suddenly, almost without waiting to choose her words, Marianne said softly, "It was foolish of you to tell me that lie about Nat the other day, Lisette."

"What lie?" Lisette's green eyes regarded Marianne with deceptive mildness, but they also narrowed very slightly, like those of a cat about to spring.

"You know quite well what I mean."

"Me, I am not a thought reader." Lisette shrugged contemptuously. "And I do not know what you are talking about."

She thinks I won't have the effrontery to put it into words, thought Marianne. And aloud, though still speaking softly, she said, "I mean that it was foolish of you to claim that Nat said he loved you. I was almost bound to find out the truth, you know."

"The truth is as I said it," Lisette asserted, and for a moment the white line of her teeth showed as she pulled back her upper lip in a curious expression of defiance. "You simply make this up because you are jealous of my success with Nat."

Even then, the offensive phrase "my success with Nat" had the power to make Marianne wince with annoyance.

"I'm making nothing up," she said coldly. "I'm merely telling you what I have now found out. I spent yesterday evening with Nat, and we had a long talk—"

"About me?" inquired the other girl quickly.

"Oh, no. You were mentioned, but only passingly," Marianne told her coolly. And although she knew she was not being very noble or high-minded about this, she felt Lisette deserved that slap. "But as I told you before, Lisette, Nat and I are old friends. We are in the habit of talking frankly to each other. I found there was no question of his being in love with you—or anyone else, incidentally."

"That is what he tells *you,*" retorted Lisette angrily. "With me it is another story."

"Well, I think not." Marianne smiled slightly, glad that she knew Nat too well to have that sort of explanation foisted off on her. "If you want to make up stories

for your own enjoyment, that's your affair. But don't
try to pass them off on me again.''

"Now it is you who are foolish,'' Lisette said, quietly
and rapidly, but with the most extraordinary intensity.
"It is not wise to make of me an enemy.'' In her anger
even the usual excellence of her English deserted her.
"You will be sorry—''

"Lisette,'' called Florian at this moment. "Come
here and stop gossiping. We need you.''

"Yes, *monsieur*.''

Lisette glided forward with an air of submission that
made the great designer glance at her suspiciously.
However, he evidently decided that whatever mischief
she was hatching had nothing to do with him, and proceeded to give directions for the pose that was needed.

Then he nodded to Marianne and said, "All right,
mademoiselle. We shall not need you. I will send these
things back when we have finished.''

So Marianne went downstairs again, wondering as
she did so if she had really been wise to speak so frankly
to Lisette and draw her angry fire. But at least there was
some satisfaction in having made a spirited attempt to
let her know she was not having everything her own
way.

On her return to the boutique, Marianne was immediately drawn into her own work again, and she thought
no more about Lisette for the next half hour.

But then Lisette came tripping down the stairs, attired
for the street—she was one of the few models who could
sometimes venture on a real lunch without any threat to
her figure—and carrying the things that had been used
in the photograph.

"Here you are, *mademoiselle*—'' she laid them
before Marianne "—*monsieur* said I was to give them to
you personally and wait while you checked them.''

Marianne proceeded to do this while Lisette stood by,
smiling slightly in that secret, pleased way that both
disturbed and irritated Marianne. "Yes. This is cor-
rect,'' she said curtly.

And, at almost the same moment, a young American

girl near her exclaimed, "Oh, my! That's Monsieur Florian himself, isn't it?"

Marianne glanced up, to see Florian coming down the stairs.

"Yes, it is." She smiled at the girl.

"Do you think he would give me his autograph?" The girl dived into an immense handbag and produced a small book. "I got the president's autograph yesterday. But it would sure make my trip if I got Monsieur Florian's, too."

"At least you could ask him," said Marianne kindly.

"I will ask him for you," declared Lisette, who loved to put herself forward, as Madame Moisant said. And as the famous designer came abreast of them, she said beguilingly, "Monsieur Florian, *madame* would be so happy if you would give her your autograph. She says she will put it beside that of the president."

"How flattering for us both," replied Florian dryly. But he smiled slightly and took out his pen.

"Oh, Monsieur Florian! This is a great moment for me," declared the delighted girl, as she handed him her book.

"For me too, *mademoiselle*," replied Florian politely. And then, "I'm sorry, my pen seems to have run out. Has anyone a pen?"

Marianne reached for hers, but Lisette was quicker.

"Here, *monsieur*—" She produced a pen from her handbag and held it out to him.

As she did so, Marianne caught her breath on an incredulous gasp. She knew that pen as well as her own, for she had given it to Nat for his birthday, only six months ago.

CHAPTER FIVE

MARIANNE HAD A momentary—and insane—impulse to snatch the pen from her employer's hand and examine it thoroughly. But, while holding herself in check from such an impossible action, she also had time to reflect that she might, after all, be mistaken. Pens are extraordinarily alike. It was just possible. . . .

But this one had a slim gold band around the top, exactly like the one she had ordered so carefully for Nat, so that his initials might be engraved upon it. There couldn't be a mistake.

Fortunately, no customer occupied her attention just then, so she could continue to follow the situation for a few seconds longer. The autograph completed, Florian handed back the book to its gratified owner and—perhaps in order to stem her too effusive thanks—he added, as he returned Lisette's pen, "It's a nice pen, Lisette. English, isn't it?"

"Yes, *monsieur*. An Englishman who is a very good friend of mine gave it to me," Lisette declared.

"So?" Florian gave her a thoughtful glance before bowing politely to the owner of the autograph book and passing on.

For a moment longer Lisette turned the pen reflectively in her hand, and as she did so Marianne clearly saw the initials N.G. engraved on the gold band. There was no further possibility of mistake. The pen was the one she had herself given to Nat.

Then Lisette replaced it in her handbag, smiled her faintly feline smile and went out into the street, leaving Marianne to cope with the jubilation of the autograph hunter.

Good training and innate politeness enabled Marianne to respond satisfactorily, but only the surface of her mind was concerned with the customer. To herself she was saying angrily—frightenedly—*What does it mean? He couldn't have given it to her. Not my pen. The one I chose so carefully for him. But if he didn't give it to her, how did she get it? Even she wouldn't actually pinch it. Or would she? She might have borrowed it, and then smilingly refused to return it. But he should have insisted! I gave it to him—and I thought he valued it for that very reason.*

At this point she was hard put to it to hold back her tears. But somehow she managed to bid her departing customer a smiling goodbye before she turned away, to stand before a drawer, pretending to put away gloves.

"What is it?" asked Marcelle quietly beside her. "You look unhappy."

"Do I? I'm trying not to," whispered Marianne in return. But then she burst out bitterly, "What would *you* feel if you'd given someone a special present and they you found he'd handed it on to someone else?"

She meant the question only rhetorically. But Marcelle immediately gave it her grave consideration.

"That depends," she said earnestly, "on how much I liked the first person."

Yes, of course, that was the point! It was because she loved Nat that the situation took on such a harrowing significance. That and the fact that it was to Lisette he had given the pen. If it had been anyone else—kind little Marcelle, for instance....

I'm getting things out of proportion, Marianne tried to tell herself. *I'm allowing the very thought of Lisette to get me rattled. But why has she Nat's pen—the pen I gave him—smugly reposing in her handbag?*

One always came back to that question. And during the rest of that busy day it stayed in Marianne's mind, a constant torment to her. From time to time she assured herself that there was a perfectly simple solution. She only had to telephone Nat that evening and ask him point-blank what the answer was.

But then she wondered if she were capable of putting

the question quite casually—not sounding as though it were a matter of life and death to her. And she was plunged into fresh despair by the realization that she now found it almost impossible to be reasonably unself-conscious about anything to do with Nat.

She hardly knew whether to be relieved or disappointed when Madame Rachel asked her to stay on later that evening as Monsieur Florian wished to discuss arrangements for the show they were to stage at the big Charities Fair, which now loomed near.

"You had no engagement for the evening, I hope?" Madame Rachel said. But it was evident that the question was purely academic. Any arrangement would have had to take second place to Monsieur Florian's requirements.

"No, *madame*," Marianne admitted, and she relinquished the idea of telephoning Nat for explanations, with something between regret and thankfulness.

After the boutique had closed for the night, she and Madame Rachel went upstairs to Monsieur Florian's office, and here they found their employer already sketching out the overall design for the stall that was to represent the Florian boutique.

"We shall be showing part of the collection during the evening," he explained. "But on this occasion it will be the boutique that will be of more immediate importance. It naturally lends itself more easily to anything like a fair."

"Undoubtedly," agreed Madame Rachel, unable to hide her satisfaction in the thought that, on this occasion at least, her part would be more distinguished than that of Madame Moisant.

"It is necessary—" Florian tapped the sketch in front of him "—to strike a good balance between a display, an advertisement and a charity stall. For though, of course, charity takes first place on this occasion, it would be idle to overlook the fact—" he smiled dryly "—that all exhibitors also regard this as a splendid opportunity for advertisement."

"Charity, as the English say, begins at home," observed Madame Rachel, firmly if not very aptly.

"In the center, here," went on Florian, refraining from taking up this much abused generalization, "we shall have the actual display that is intended to attract attention. Nothing will be for sale in this section, but it will represent the absolute flower of our costume jewelry."

"You mean—the pick of what we have in the boutique, *monsieur*?" inquired Marianne, leaning over with enormous interest, to regard the sketch.

"Not only that. One or two of our regular customers have offered to lend specially beautiful pieces that they have bought from us in the past. In fact—" he shrugged, as though not altogether pleased "—my wife insists on lending, as the centerpiece, the brooch that I gave her as a wedding present."

"The rose spray, you mean?" Madame Rachel's tone hovered between pleasure and consternation. "It will be a great responsibility."

"I think so, too. But—" he shrugged again "—Gabrielle insists. And, of course, it will make a wonderful exhibit."

"Is it so beautiful?" Marianne looked from one to the other with a smile of genuine interest.

"The most beautiful piece of costume jewelry ever produced in Paris," Madame Rachel said solemnly. "And that, of course," she added, "is to say the most beautiful produced anywhere."

"It's very lovely," Monsieur Florian agreed, more moderately. "But—to continue." He turned back to the sketch. "On either side, and to the front, we shall have the things that are actually for sale. The prices will be slightly higher than usual, since the whole thing is for charity. And we, of course, will take only a nominal profit, as our contribution. This will mean repricing everything for the occasion. You understand, *mademoiselle*?"

"Yes, *monsieur*," Marianne said obediently.

"It will also mean at least two very late nights for those taking part. Both the night before the fair, when all is arranged, ready for display, and then on the night of the fair itself. We shall sell during the intervals of the Opéra Gala, and also at the end of the performance. I wish to have you as Madame Rachel's chief assistant. I hope that is agreeable to you?"

"Why, of course, *monsieur*!" Marianne wondered what would have happened if she had said it was not agreeable to her.

"*Bon!* We shall dress you, of course, for the occasion," added Monsieur Florian almost carelessly, and Marianne gave a little gasp of excited pleasure.

"How wonderful!"

"Well—" Florian gave that faintly indulgent smile "—you also will be part of our advertisement. You will be wearing evening dress, naturally. And I think—" he studied her thoughtfully "—I think number seventeen in the collection will be the right one for you."

"Number seventeen?"

"She is not yet experienced," explained Madame Rachel, with the good-humored air of one apologizing for a child who had forgotten her party piece. "She does not remember the dresses by number. It is the gray, with the gold tracery. The line is classic and the draped—"

"Oh, yes, I know! It was a wonderful dress!" exclaimed Marianne, with an enthusiasm that drew a smile from both of her employers. "Monsieur Florian, do you really mean that I'm going to wear that?"

"I think so. We will have a faintly bluer gray for you, and the gold must be the real corn gold of your hair. You should do us credit, *mademoiselle*."

"Oh, Monsieur Florian, I'll try to."

"Is the Englishman coming to the fair?" inquired Florian, with an air of simple curiosity that people found endearing or maddening, according to whether they liked Florian or not.

"The—Englishman, *monsieur*?"

"The one who owned the pen," explained Florian unexpectedly.

"*Monsieur*—h-how did you know?"

"Monsieur Florian knows everything," observed

Madame Rachel, as though taking some sort of credit for that herself.

"You flatter me, *madame*," murmured Florian. "I do a little inspired guessing. That is all. And after one has observed the world as long as I have, it is easier to make two and two into four than it is for some other people. I think you must arrange that he comes, *mademoiselle*. You will undoubtedly be looking your most attractive."

Marianne laughed a little protestingly and flushed. "I will see what I can do, *monsieur*," she said.

Madame Rachel looked faintly curious, but refrained from asking questions. Not from lack of inquisitiveness, but because, unlike Florian himself, she considered it slightly beneath her dignity to show interest in the private concern of her *vendeuses*.

Further details were discussed at some length. Then, when Monsieur Florian was satisfied that both Madame Rachel and Marianne had the whole thing very clearly in their minds, he dismissed them both with a word of apology for having taken up so much of their own time.

"Our time is yours, *monsieur*," declared Madame Rachel somewhat falsely, for she could grumble as much as the next one, really, if she thought she was being imposed upon.

Perhaps Florian knew that, for he gave a grim little smile as the two rose to go. But, whereas Madame Rachel went out of the room immediately, Marianne lingered for a daring moment and asked impulsively, even breathlessly, "*Monsieur*, how did you know that the pen belonged to—to Nat?"

"So the name is Nat? *Ma foi*, what a name for a hero!" exclaimed the Frenchman disgustedly. "I did not know that he was Nat, *mon enfant*. Only you yourself more or less told me that you and Lisette were interested in the same man. When I saw Lisette twirling the pen and talking of her English friend, and looking like the small cat who has eaten the canary of someone else, it did not take great intelligence to realize that this was her way of taunting a rival. And you, *mademoiselle*, were not proof against it. You looked pale and distressed."

"Did I?" Marianne was chagrined. "I—I had hoped I hid the fact that I was taken aback."

"From most people, perhaps. But not from me," stated Florian, with curiously inoffensive pleasure in his own perspicacity. "But have courage, *mademoiselle*. Number seventeen will do a great deal for you. See that Nat—" again he made a slight face "—is present at the Charities Fair."

Marianne laughed. "I will, *monsieur*. But—Lisette will also be at the Charities Fair, no doubt?"

"To be sure," said Florian, with a shrug. "But in number seventeen you will not exactly be at a disadvantage. Good night, *mademoiselle*."

And, seeing that she had now presumed as far as was wise, Marianne bade her employer good night and went downstairs. Here she found Madame Rachel on the point of departure. But that lady paused to give her a sharp glance and say coldly, "A good *vendeuse*, like a well-behaved child, speaks when spoken to, Marianne. You must not think that, because Monsieur Florian occasionally interests himself personally, one may take the liberties."

"No, *madame*, I didn't think that," Marianne assured her humbly.

"Good. Then we understand ourselves," said Madame Rachel somewhat ambiguously, and made a good exit.

When Marianne reached home it was not really as late as she had expected, and since she had the unusual luxury of a telephone in her own room, she decided all at once that she would telephone Nat after all.

I'll ask him if he's coming to the Charities Fair, she thought. *And then, somehow, I'll casually introduce the subject of Lisette—and the pen.* Though, as she dialed his number with a slightly unsteady hand, she knew perfectly well that "casually" was only a manner of speaking.

The bell at the other end rang so long that she feared he must be out. But then, just as she was about to give up the attempt, Nat's voice said abstractedly, "Yes? What is it?"

"Oh, Nat—it's Marianne. Am I calling too late?"

"No, of course not. What sort of time is it, anyway? I haven't been noticing. I've been busy on an article."

"Then I shouldn't really interrupt you—"

"It's all right. I'm stuck, so I'm glad of a distraction. What have you been doing with yourself this evening?"

"Working late," explained Marianne, happy to be a welcome distraction. "We've been discussing plans for our exhibit at the Charities Fair. Do you know about it?"

"On the fourteenth, isn't it? At the Opéra. A very big affair, I understand."

"Yes. I wondered if you'd be covering it for your paper."

"Well, it isn't quite up my alley, but I might work it into something, I suppose. Lisette was anxious for me to come."

"Was she?" said Marianne. And, all at once, a cold fury took possession of her. She was sick of the sound of that name—of everything it implied—of all the misery that the owner of it seemed able to inflict upon her. And, without even pausing to think how unwisely she was acting, she went on, "Oh, yes—and speaking of Lisette reminds me—how does she come to be in possession of your pen?"

"My pen?" She was almost certain she heard a subtle change in his tone. "What pen?"

"You know perfectly well what pen!" The prevarication only added fuel to her anger. "The one I gave you. I chose it especially for you, and had your initials engraved on it. And now there's Lisette, smirking around the boutique and openly displaying *my* pen!"

"Mine, you mean," Nat said coldly. "I thought you gave it to me."

"Well, I did! That's why—" Marianne caught herself up and bit her lip, divided between a desire to cry and a desire to go on telling Nat just what she thought of him. "Look, Nat—" she made a tremendous effort to be calm and dignified ''—you must understand how I feel about this. There was—''

''And how about the way I feel at this moment,'' his voice interrupted dryly, ''with you berating me over the phone like this. I thought we were amicably discussing the Charities Fair, and suddenly I find myself more or less in the dock over a fountain pen.''

''Not just *a* fountain pen!'' Again she strove to sound calm. ''I chose it especially—''

''You've said that before,'' he told her impatiently.

''But, Nat, surely you understand. No one likes to see a—a gift of theirs passed on to someone else, as though it's of no value.''

''Oh, Marianne, for heaven's sake! All this fuss about a pen!''

She was struck silent with dismay, too confused and unhappy in that moment to be able to decide whether it were he or she who was being unreasonable. Then, steadying her voice with some difficulty, she said, ''I'm sorry if I'm making too much of this. But one simply doesn't give away a friend's present to someone else, in that casual manner.''

''Who says I gave it to her, in a casual manner?'' he retorted impatiently.

''Well, she has it, doesn't she?'' cried Marianne, beside herself with indignation and distress. ''There she is, flaunting it around. The pen that I gave you—that you might have set a little value on—that—''

Suddenly she stopped speaking, aware that there was a chilling silence at the other end.

''N—Nat,'' she said timidly. And then, more urgently, ''*Nat!*''

But there was no answer. Then, slowly, the incredible truth was borne in upon her. There was no one listening. Nat had quietly replaced his receiver.

''Oh, no!'' She actually shook her own receiver before, realizing how ridiculous this was. Then she slowly put it back on its stand.

''What has happened to us?'' she said aloud, though in a whisper, and she sat down on the side of her bed and rubbed her hands together as though they were cold. "We never spoke to each other like that before. I—I almost shouted at him—like a common shrew."

She wiped away a few tears with the backs of her hands.

"I shouldn't have spoken so. But then, he should have been frank with me! Why couldn't he just say, 'I gave it to her. I'm sorry. I shouldn't have done it, but—' and then given a reason—any reason—for what he'd done?

"Oh, it's too absurd and horrible! All about a pen. That's what he said himself. Only he made it sound as though I shouldn't have minded. Perhaps I shouldn't. Perhaps I should call him and apologize—"

Her hand went out toward the telephone, but she drew it back. To call again now would savor of pestering him. Besides, she had her pride. Nat still had not explained about giving Lisette that wretched pen, and it was he who had rudely cut the conversation short.

She would have to wait a day or two before she made any attempt at reconciliation. And perhaps—oh, surely—before then he would himself make some friendly approach.

FOR A WHILE Marianne buoyed herself up with this hope. It served to sustain her during most of the following day. But after that, both hopes and spirits drooped unbearably.

A dozen times she was tempted to call Nat up and make some sort of apology, but a dozen times she resisted. It was not until three evenings later, with her spirits at their lowest ebb, that she finally capitulated. And then, although she let the phone ring for a long, long time, there was no reply. Inexpressibly chilled, she gave it up after that.

Once more—as when she had been unable to get in touch with him earlier—it would have been even more unbearable if she had not had the excitement of her work to take her mind off her personal troubles. Apart from all the business that the new collection brought to the boutique, there was the question of selecting and discussing what was to be shown on the stall at the Charities Fair.

Marianne had to be fitted with her dress. And, although it was probable that Nat would now never see her in it, she could not be less than entranced by the picture she presented in it.

Florian had been quite right, as usual. The dress might have been inspired by and designed for her, and Florian himself expressed extreme satisfaction when he saw her in it.

"It is perfect." He walked around her, viewing her from every angle.

"I've never worn anything so marvelous in my life before," Marianne told him frankly.

"No, of course not," he said, just as frankly. And he looked faintly surprised when Marianne laughed.

"We are supporting charities well," was the dry comment of Madame Rachel, who in her dignified, faintly austere way also looked superb in the dress Florian had chosen for her.

During all this time Marianne had seen nothing of Roger Senloe. She knew that he was away in Geneva, and she missed him more than she could have believed possible. If only he had been there, she thought she could have told him about the contretemps with Nat and asked him if he thought she had been unreasonable.

Somehow, one *could* tell Roger Senloe things. There was something humorously impersonal about him that made it easy. Besides, after the time he had found her crying on a bench, it was no good starting to be inhibited with him. In some ways he knew more about her than almost anyone else.

On the evening before the Charities Fair, Marianne accompanied Monsieur Florian and Madame Rachel to the Opéra. And for the first time she was able to see what a superb setting this was going to be for the fair.

The great mirrored hall, where the audience would promenade in the intervals, had already been decorated—simply and yet almost with drama, as only the

Parisians can decorate. Arc lights had been installed on the grand staircase, ready to shine upon ascending celebrities, and the great red carpet was ready to be rolled out, not only down the staircase, but outside the Opéra, down the steps, to the very edge of the sidewalk.

"Twenty girls from the top families of France will sell the program," Madame Rachel explained to Marianne. "And there—" she indicated a small balcony "—is where the trumpeters will stand, to sound a fanfare for the most celebrated of the guests."

"It looks wonderful already," Marianne declared.

"Tomorrow, with all the lights and dresses, it will look a thousand times more wonderful," Madame Rachel confidently prophesied. "Come, now we must get to work."

In the great mirrored hall the bare stands had been set up. And with incredible speed and skill Florian himself carried out the blending and draping of exquisite materials, until the skeleton stand was transformed into an exotically beautiful background for the things from the boutique.

Marianne's part consisted in little more than standing by, ready to hand whatever her employer required. But she was so completely absorbed in even this minor role that she had no eyes for anything else, until a familiar voice beside her said, "Very glamorous, I must say. And what's your part in this?"

"Oh—Roger! How nice!" She turned, smiling, to find both Roger Senloe and Madame Florian surveying the now almost completed stall. "I didn't know you'd be back in time."

"I got in this afternoon. You know Marianne Shore, don't you, Gabrielle?"

"Yes, indeed." Gabrielle Florian greeted Marianne kindly, and then turned to her husband. "I brought along the rose spray, Georges, in case you wanted to see how it looked."

"It will not be needed until tomorrow," Florian murmured abstractedly. "None of the valuable stuff will be left here overnight."

"I know. But I thought you might like to see the effect—"

"Yes, yes." Gently but firmly, Florian put her out of his way, a little as though he had not really noticed who she was, and went on with his work.

Gabrielle Florian shrugged, laughed and turned to the other two.

"We came too soon," she remarked to Roger. "For half an hour longer we still don't exist."

"It won't be long now, *madame*," Marianne said, with a smile. "And meanwhile, please could I see the rose spray? I've heard such a lot about it, but I've never seen it."

"Why, of course." Obligingly, Gabrielle opened a jewel case she was holding, and Marianne exclaimed aloud with admiration and delight.

"I usually wear it as a shoulder brooch, on a black evening dress," Madame Florian explained, turning the case this way and that, so that the light caught the brilliants and struck curious shafts of color from them.

It was quite a large spray and beautifully fashioned. But what made it particularly lovely was that the flowers and leaves were poised on such delicate stems of platinum wire that they actually trembled and shifted, as though they had some life of their own.

"I've never seen anything like it before," Marianne said.

"It's very unusual. That's why I felt I should lend it for this occasion. My husband was rather against the idea, and, I believe, Madame Rachel, too."

"But we'll take the greatest care of it," Marianne promised.

"I'm sure you will," Gabrielle Florian said with a smile.

And then her husband seemed to become aware of her, and called her to his side to give her opinion about something, and Marianne and Roger were left alone together for a few moments.

"Well, how's boutique life?" he inquired, smiling down at her indulgently.

"Wonderful. I'm enjoying it immensely."

"That's fine. And—everything else?"

"Well...." Even there, in the midst of the preparations for the Charities Fair, Marianne was tempted to start pouring out her troubles to him, for that was the effect this big, smiling Englishman seemed to have upon her. But recollecting just in time that this was no place for extended confidences, she contented herself with saying, "Not quite smooth sailing. But I'm hoping to—to clear things up soon. I'll—I'll tell you another time."

"Will you really? I'm flattered."

"Why?" asked Marianne simply.

"That you place so much confidence in me, I suppose."

"Oh—that? It seems the natural thing to do. I mean—"

"No, don't explain it away," he begged her with a laugh. "That's a very nice compliment. I had no idea anyone valued my discretion and judgment so highly."

"But of course they do! Ask Madame Florian," Marianne told him.

But he smiled and shook his head slightly.

"I—think not. Not nowadays," he said. And for a moment he glanced across, with a sort of impatient tenderness, toward the fair-haired girl who was in such earnest colloquy with Florian.

Why, thought Marianne, in sudden wondering realization, *he's still in love with her!* And somehow the discovery gave her a slight shock.

No one stayed very long after that. Florian expressed himself as satisfied with the arrangements, as far as they could take them at this point, and Marianne and Madame Rachel were sent home, with the injunction to come in an hour later in the morning, as there was no knowing how late they would be working the following evening.

To complete Marianne's pleasure, she was given an extra pass for the fair, and this she decided to hand on to her American neighbor, who had so ardently wanted to go when she first mentioned the occasion.

"You angel! You little gold-plated angel!" cried Sadie, embracing her when the ticket was handed over. "I've been dying to go, but couldn't possibly rustle up the money for it. Do you really mean that, out of all Paris, you're going to let me have this?"

"Yes, certainly." Marianne laughed, and reflected that, out of all Paris, there were very few people she knew well enough to invite. There would have been Nat, of course, if only—"

"Don't any of your colleagues want it? Not that I'm going to give it up, now that I'm actually clutching it in my hot little hand," declared Sadie.

"They have chances of other things," Marianne said. "Except—" She stopped suddenly, thinking remorsefully of Marcelle.

"Don't remember any deserving exceptions now," begged Sadie. "It isn't any good."

"It wouldn't be any good, in any case," Marianne said, smilingly shaking her head. "This one has a patient and demanding mother, I understand, who probably wouldn't let her go."

"Preserve me from that sort of parent!" exclaimed Sadie fervently. "Thank heavens mine is back in Wisconsin, and much too busy to be either patient or demanding."

But, when Marianne arrived at the boutique the following morning, it appeared that Monsieur Florian could even take patient and demanding mothers in his stride. For a flushed and sparkling Marcelle greeted her rapturously.

"Imagine! I too am to go to the fair—and sell at the boutique stall. Monsieur Florian has decided it at the very last moment, so that *maman* has not even time to be ill about it. I mean—" she caught herself up guiltily "—only this morning she said she was feeling better. Monsieur Florian himself telephoned her and explained that he needed another *vendeuse*, after all, and that he wanted it to be me. And I am to wear number sixty-four in the collection, because it fits me almost exactly. Isn't it wonderful?"

"Absolutely marvelous!" declared Marianne, from her heart. And she actually kissed Marcelle in her enthusiasm.

After that everything was excitement and gaiety. The usual effervescing atmosphere in both fashion house and boutique threatened to erupt at any moment in volcanic proportions, and only cold applications of common sense administered from time to time by Madame Moisant served to quell actual hysteria.

Even so, everything was completed in order and on time. The collection received its daily showing, customers were welcomed, dealt with and wafted on their way, and finally, at the appointed time, Marianne and Marcelle, attired in their Florian finery, went by taxi to the Opéra, where Monsieur Florian and Madame Rachel had completed the arrangement of the boutique stall.

Everything was now in order. And as the mirrored walls gave back endless reflections of the colorful scene, Marianne thought she had never seen anything more beautiful in her life.

"But ours is the loveliest of all," declared Marcelle, in a very partisan sort of way. "The other stalls are nice. But no one has a hand like Monsieur Florian."

Marianne was fain to agree. And as the first visitors began to arrive, the stall representing the Florian boutique began to be one of the chief centers of attraction. Many greeted Madame Rachel as an old friend, and from time to time the models from Florian's would drift up to exult with childish openness in the superiority of "their" stall.

Even Lisette lingered admiringly for some time. And she took the opportunity to say, with insolent carelessness to Marianne, "Nat will not come until later. I told him the collection will not be shown until midnight."

"Did you?" returned Marianne coldly, and somehow she contrived to hide her mingled eagerness and uneasiness in the thought that Nat *was* coming, after all.

She was kept pretty busy, for Madame Rachel had explained that she herself would often have to spend a while being gracious and social to a customer, and that during that time, Marianne must consider herself in charge.

Marcelle proved unexpectedly helpful. But, even so, whenever Madame Rachel sauntered away from the stall with someone—which she did from time to time—Marianne felt her responsibilites weigh heavily upon her.

On the other hand, there was so much to amuse and delight one, simply in glancing around. And then, during one of those intervals of her being left in charge, her roving glance fell on a familiar figure. Only some yards away, though a gap in the crowd, she saw Nat—and he was looking straight at her, an expression of almost wondering admiration on his face.

And suddenly she knew that, in the Florian dress, she had impinged on his consciousness for the very first time as a beautiful girl in her own right. Not as Yvonne's sister. Not as a "wonderful confidante and safety valve," but as Marianne.

"Nat!" Forgetting everything else, she went quickly toward him, aware that this was the moment for putting everything right.

"Marianne, you look absolutely stunning!" He caught her hands in his. "Gosh! I'd no idea you were such a beauty."

"Oh, thank you." She laughed for sheer happiness. "It's the dress, really."

"It's nothing of the sort. It's you. Let's get out of this bedlam and go somewhere where we can talk."

"No, I can't. I'm in charge—" Suddenly she remembered her responsibilities and actually turned to go. But he held her hand tightly still.

"You can't go yet. I must talk to you. Marianne, I'm confoundedly sorry about the other evening—"

"Oh, it was my fault, too! I shouldn't have nagged you. I was so ashamed of myself afterward."

"You didn't need to be. I deserved to be kicked. I meant to explain—"

"Nat dear, it doesn't matter. Nothing matters if we're friends again."

"Doesn't it?" he said slowly. "Is that really how you feel?"

"Yes, of course. Only—I must go. I simply must go, Nat. I'm not supposed to leave the stall while Madame Rachel is away. Marcelle can't cope on her own."

"But when can I see you to talk to you properly?"

"Perhaps later. If not, call me up tomorrow evening. Oh, Nat, I'm so happy to be friends again! Only let me go now."

He laughed at that and drew her quickly against him and kissed her before he let her go.

He had kissed her sometimes before, of course, only in a brotherly sort of way. This was not in a brotherly way. And as she almost ran back to the stall, she seemed to feel the firm, warm touch of his lips still on her cheek.

She was happy and bewildered and remorseful, all at the same time, but the one thing that mattered was that she and Nat were friends again. Perhaps—more than friends.

To a flustered Marcelle, who was trying to cope with two customers at once, she murmured a contrite apology. Then, automatically, she cast a quick, comprehensive glance over the stall. It all looked lovely still. Everything—

And then suddenly she gave a gasp of incredulous horror.

Not all of it looked lovely still. In the center stood an empty velvet stand. Madame Florian's rose spray brooch had disappeared.

CHAPTER SIX

FOR ONE FRIGHTFUL, panic-stricken moment, Marianne really thought she was going to faint. Then her heart began to pound in slow, heavy thuds, and she felt the blood being pumped back into her pale face. But she still stood there, transfixed by the sight of that empty stand.

"What is it? For heaven's sake, Marianne, what is wrong?" Marcelle, free now from the importunities of her two customers, came to stand at her side. "Have you had bad news or something?"

"It's—the brooch." Marianne found she had a curious difficulty in forming words. "Look! Madame Florian's rose spray brooch is gone!"

"Nonsense! It can't be!" A curious, almost greenish pallor spread over Marcelle's face, and for a moment Marianne regretted having drawn her attention to what had happened. But the shock would have been the same if she had suddenly noted the loss for herself.

"But it was there—not five minutes ago," Marcelle whispered. "And only I was at the stall serving. They'll say it was my fault," she added, with the hopeless certainty of one who was used to blame.

"No, they won't," Marianne asserted stoutly. "The fault was mine. I was in charge while Madame Rachel was away. It was my responsibility. I shouldn't have left the stall."

"Then why did you leave the stall?" Marcelle asked distractedly.

"I went to speak to a—a friend."

"Was that all?" Marcelle sounded incredulous.

"It was rather important to me. But never mind that now. The point is—what are we to do? It—it couldn't have slipped down, could it?"

In the forlorn hope that it might have done so, the two girls probed anxiously among the other things on the stall, but with no result. At the same time, they had to preserve a semblance of all being well, and be ready to attend to any customer who might choose to stop.

Fortunately, at this point, repeated fanfares from the grand staircase proclaimed the fact that the really distinguished guests were arriving. With one accord the crowds began to make for the stairs, and Marianne and Marcelle had a few minutes in which to consider what they could do.

"You didn't notice anyone pausing unduly long near the stall, I suppose?" Marianne asked hopelessly.

"Not really. How could I? I was busy serving. But of course there were people coming and going all the time. It—it could have been any of them. Except that surely no one would steal on an occasion like this?"

Marianne was silent, unable to share this charitable supposition.

"How are we going to tell Madame Rachel?" Marcelle was nearly crying. "And, still more, Monsieur Florian?"

"Let me worry about that," Marianne said resolutely. "You're in no way to blame, Marcelle. And I'll see no one goes for you."

"But why should you?" The other girl still seemed unable to believe in the possibility of being cleared.

"Because I'm not in the least like your patient *maman*," retorted Marianne bluntly. "If only I knew—"

And then, with a feeling of immense, if illogical, relief, she saw Roger Senloe making his way toward them.

She signalled urgently to him, and as soon as he came within speaking distance she exclaimed, "Oh, Roger, thank heaven you've come! Something awful has happened."

"What? One of the other designers set up a better exhibit than Florian? My word, you girls look attractive!"

"Never mind that now! I mean something really awful. Madame Florian's rose brooch has disappeared—been stolen.''

"Good Lord!" Immediately his lazily indulgent smile changed to something like consternation, and his glance went to the empty stand. "Does Florian know?''

"N-no," said Marianne uncertainly. "No one knows yet except us. It's only just happened.''

"When you were both busy selling?"

For a moment Marianne was most sorely tempted to say a simple yes to that. If she did so, no one could blame her. She could take refuge in the story that, like Marcelle, she had been too busy to notice what was happening. Madame Florian had taken a calculated risk in lending her brooch. She had just been unlucky.

But—she glanced at Roger's grave face—one didn't tell lies to Roger. Nor to Florian, come to that. The sorry truth had to be told.

"I wasn't selling," she said deliberately. "The responsibility is mine, I'm afraid. I left the stall, in Madame Rachel's absence, which I was not supposed to do. I ran across to . . . to speak to Nat. And when I came back the brooch had gone. It wasn't Marcelle's fault. She had to attend to two customers because I was missing. She couldn't do any more.''

"I should perhaps have kept better watch," Marcelle suggested, timidly but loyally.

"You couldn't do more than you did," persisted Marianne stubbornly.

"That seems a pretty fair statement," agreed Roger gravely. "Where is Madame Rachel?''

"I'm not very sure. One of the real VIPs wanted her, and she left me in charge. That was when it happened.''

"Then I'd better get hold of Florian. He'll have to know eventually, and the fewer intermediaries the better. I suppose the thing was insured, along with everything else here. But of course it's the sentimental value that one can't replace.''

"I know," Marianne said dejectedly.

"Well, cheer up. I'll find Florian. And if Madame

Rachel comes back first, I'd be inclined not to rush into explanations. She may not notice the loss at once."

Roger went away, and the two girls made another forlorn search, which was interrupted by the return of Madame Rachel, in a brisk and cheerful mood.

"All goes very well," she observed to her two young *vendeuses*, who secretly thought that all went very badly. "It is a pity that one cannot also hear the performance, but this is not what we are here for. I peeped into the house from one of the upper boxes, and the scene was splendid. Indeed, in Paris we know how to put on a gala!"

"Yes, *madame*," agreed Marianne with an effort, while Marcelle could not even produce a simple word of agreement.

"Have you been busy?" The director of the boutique swept an all-seeing glance over her two assistants and their stall. As she did so, she emitted a sharp little scream, and Marianne found herself wondering why on earth they had supposed that the empty stand would escape Madame Rachel's eagle glance.

"The rose brooch!" she gasped. "Madame Florian's brooch! It is gone!"

"Yes, *madame*," said Marianne again. "We—we have just discovered the loss."

"You have just discovered it! And you stand there saying, 'Yes, *madame*,' and 'No, *madame*,' as though nothing has happened!" cried the infuriated director—inaccurately, for no one yet had dared to say, "No, *madame*."

"You must be mad!" she went on, her voice rising a couple of tones. "Do you realize what *monsieur* will say,—what he will do? That brooch was a wedding present from him to Madame Florian. It was of immense value to them both. He may dismiss us all for incompetence. And you remain calm and—"

"Madame Rachel, I don't feel in the least calm," Marianne interrupted quietly. "If you want to know, I feel rather sick. But there is no question of our all being sacked for incompetence. You, at least, were not even here. Monsieur Florian is a reasonable man—"

"Monsieur Florian, like all men, is not reasonable when he is angry," declared Madame Rachel. "He can be a fiend—a monster—at such times."

Used as she was to the exaggerations and dramatics of her world, Marianne blanched slightly at this prospect, and poor Marcelle actually uttered a slight sob.

"Well, we shall soon see," said Marianne, as calmly as she could, "Mr. Senloe has gone to find Monsieur Florian, and they should be here any minute now."

"Monsieur Senloe knows about it?" Madame Rachel became a little less excited. "And he has gone for Monsieur Florian?"

"Yes, *madame*."

"Pray heaven he finds him before he goes into the theater itself." Madame Rachel cast up her fine eyes, as though drawing heaven's special attention to this plea. "The overture must be about to begin."

But evidently the efficient Roger had found Florian in time. For at this moment they both entered the great mirrored hall, and with them came Gabrielle Florian herself, attired in a fantastically beautiful dress of peacock-blue brocade.

There was a grim air about Florian, and Marianne found herself trembling as the three approached.

"*Monsieur*, I am appalled—desolated," exclaimed Madame Rachel, as they came up. "I have only just heard the story from these foolish girls, and—"

"All right, *madame*. I will now hear the story myself," interrupted Florian curtly. "Tell me what happened, *mademoiselle*." And he fixed Marianne with such a cold and steely glare that she was uncomfortably reminded of Madame Rachel's saying that he could be a monster on these occasions.

Even so, she strove to keep her voice steady as she said, "I'm afraid the fault was mine, *monsieur*." She heard Madame Rachel gasp, but whether at the stupidity or the effrontery of this statement it was not possible to say. And then she went on to tell him, as she had told Roger, what had happened.

"You mean—you left the stall and went to speak to someone? A customer?"

"No, *monsieur*. A private friend," Marianne said resolutely.

"Had you any instructions as to what you were to do when Madame Rachel was absent?"

"Yes, *monsieur*."

"Just a moment." Florian put up his hand to stop the eager words that were obviously trembling on Madame Rachel's indignant lips. "*Mademoiselle* will answer for herself. What were those instructions?"

Roger Senloe shifted from one foot to the other and began to look oddly sullen.

"I was to be responsible for the stall, and I was not to leave it until *madame* returned."

"*Voilà!*" exclaimed Madame Rachel triumphantly.

"But you deliberately disobeyed those instructions?"

"Look here, Florian, I think—" began Roger Senloe.

"Allow me to deal with my own staff," Florian said coldly, and even Roger subsided into silence, though reluctantly. "Well, *mademoiselle*, you deliberately disobeyed your instructions?"

"Monsieur Florian, it was not deliberate," Marianne explained unhappily. "I just didn't think—"

"*Mademoiselle*, I have no room in my firm for people who just do not think. Thanks to your disobedience and thoughtlessness—"

"Georges," said the girl in the peacock-blue dress and she lightly took him by the arm so that she was much more difficult to ignore than either Roger Senloe or Madame Rachel, "I should like to ask one question."

"Very well." Florian shrugged impatiently. But although he did not even glance at his wife, something about him insensibly softened at her touch.

"Marianne," said Gabrielle Florian, and the friendly, intimate use of her Christian name brought a sudden lump into Marianne's throat, "was it very important that you should speak to this friend of yours?"

"Well, it—it was rather," Marianne admitted, a little huskily.

"In fact, it was an opportunity not to be missed?"

"I—I thought so."

"Then that's the answer. We all do these things occasionally," said Gabrielle Florian, looking around at the others. "We've all been madly sorry for something, or ready to kick ourselves when it's too late. As a matter of fact, I was wrong to insist on lending the brooch. It was too much of a responsibility for other people. You said so at the time, Georges. You were right, as usual."

"But...one moment." For once Florian refused to respond to his wife's coaxing smile. "I'm afraid one cannot leave it there."

"But I *have* left it there," retorted Gabrielle smiling still. "And it's my brooch we're dealing with."

"We are also dealing with my staff," returned her husband grimly. "And—"

"Don't be tiresome, *mon cher*," said Gabrielle. "Remember the incident of the green dress."

"What green dress?" inquired Florian disagreeably.

But Roger Senloe laughed suddenly and said, almost genially, "To be sure! It has a certain parallel."

"You know perfectly well what green dress," Gabrielle told her husband calmly. "The green dress that I borrowed for the collection without permission, and that got wine spilled all over it. You were even more furious with me than you are now with Mademoiselle Marianne. But later you admitted you were wrong, and you gave me the dress. Remember?"

"Yes, of course I remember. But that has nothing whatever to do with the present occasion."

"It has, in a way. Because that was when I fell in love with you," Gabrielle said on a note of calm reflection. "And if I hadn't fallen in love with you, I wouldn't have married you. And if I hadn't married you, you wouldn't have given me the brooch—and none of this would have happened."

"Is that what you call logic?" inquired her husband with a reluctant laugh.

"No. It was only meant to make you laugh—which it has done. But the real point of the story is that sometimes, even if people have done something quite wrong under strong compulsion, one must understand and forgive them. Particularly if they make no attempt to evade the issue. It is not easy to tell an unpalatable truth to you, Georges. I know! Mademoiselle Marianne was brave to admit her fault. It would have been equally easy to say she had not left the stall, but that she had been too busy to notice what was happening."

"It seems to me," growled Florian, "that you are putting too high a value on a simple statement of truth."

"The simple truth is not told so often in our world," replied his wife dryly. "And this you know as well as I do."

There was a moment's silence. Then Florian said rather disagreeably, "Then what do you want me to do?"

"Nothing, really," replied Gabrielle with a quick smile at Marianne. "Except that I suppose you should report the loss to the police who are on duty here. But I'm afraid—" just for a moment her lip trembled "—I have seen the last of my rose spray brooch."

"Madame Florian," Marianne said in a low voice, "you are being most extraordinarily generous. I simply don't know how to thank you."

"Well, find some way of doing so," exclaimed Florian curtly. "For without her intervention you would have been dismissed from my employ."

"I know, *monsieur*." And Marianne tightly clasped the hand that Gabrielle held out to her.

"One gets over everything in time," observed Gabrielle, with an impartial glance around. "And now perhaps we can slip into our box in time for the end of the first act. Are you coming, Roger?"

It seemed, after a second's hesitation, that Roger was. And as Marianne looked after the three, she thought, No wonder he's still in love with her!

"You are a fortunate girl," observed Madame Rachel acidly, by way of bringing her back to earth.

"I know it, *madame*," said Marianne earnestly.

"If Madame Florian had not been here, it would have gone very badly for you."

"Madame Florian is an angel from heaven!" exclaimed Marcelle emotionally.

"She knows how to manage Monsieur Florian—which is even more important," replied Madame Rachel, with a short laugh that showed that she was gradually returning to her usual state of comparative good humor.

After that, the rest of the evening seemed almost uneventful. In a somewhat subdued mood, Marianne and Marcelle dealt with the flow of customers who came to their stall during the intermissions and for the half hour that the fair remained open after the gala performance was over.

At twelve-thirty, however, the stalls closed, the small amount of merchandise remaining was packed away, and the hall was cleared for the final models' parade that was to close the evening's proceedings.

The top five designers, in an atmosphere of false smiles and bitter rivalry, had combined to put on a superb show, consisting of the forty dresses that each considered to be the flower of his collection.

Here Lisette at last came into her own. And here at last the two girls from the boutique found that they could sit down and rest their aching feet and watch someone else work, without any uneasy feeling that they were not attending to their own responsibilities.

Just before the show began, someone slipped into the empty seat beside Marianne, and Nat's voice whispered, "Well, at last here's a chance of speaking to you!"

"Oh, Nat, hello!" She turned her head and smiled at him. "Have you had a nice evening?"

"Pretty good. With two terrific highlights. One was Peroni's singing of the *Addio*, and the other was my first glimpse of you in that stunning dress."

"You're going to see lots of other stunning dresses now," she reminded him.

"The girl inside makes something of a difference, though." And though she did not look at him at that moment, she knew from the sound of his voice that he was smiling reminiscently.

"Yes, of course," she said. And then, still without looking at him, "You're going to see Lisette in one of the most fantastic dresses that even Florian ever created."

"Am I? So what?"

"N-nothing. Except that I thought you'd be interested."

"Never mind about Lisette now. Marianne—are you still mad at me about that pen?"

"N-not really. Not if there's an explanation."

"Maybe it will sound feeble to you. But I lent it to her to write down something I wanted—and we were fooling around rather—and it was before I'd met up with you again. In a way, I thought that chapter was over. I was feeling sore and silly about Yvonne—and in some stupid way I seemed to attach the same feeling to you. Can you understand or does it all seem too silly?"

"No, I think I understand," Marianne said gently.

"Well, then, she—Lisette—took a fancy to the pen, and wanted to keep it. I didn't really want her to have it, but I guess I didn't insist firmly enough. Anyway, it ended with her hanging on to it. And then, when you asked about it, I knew I'd been in the wrong and—"

"Oh, Nat dear, you don't have to say anything else at all." Silently she slipped her hand into his. "If there's any apologizing to be done, I should be apologizing, too. I behaved very badly the other night. Berating you like—like a fishwife."

"Not at all like a fishwife," he told her in an amused whisper. "Just like a freeborn British lass, standing up to her man in a way that's good for him."

Then someone said, "Ssh, ssh," and the first announcement was made and the show began.

But Marianne hardly saw the first half dozen designs. She was aware only of Nat's hand in hers, and of that queer way he had described her as "standing up to her man in a way that's good for him."

Did he just mean that in a general way of speaking? Or had he really been wishing to identify himself as "her man"?

It was impossible to say. But even to speculate on such an enchanting theme made her happy. Worn out by the varying emotions of the evening, lulled by the sense of contentment that his nearness gave her, she sat there almost in a dream, watching the glamorous figures of the models pass and repass.

Until Lisette appeared. And then a sudden sharpening of all her senses literally made her sit up straighter.

Lisette made her very first appearance in the strangely beautiful red and green dress, and as she glided past, people leaned forward as though some almost magnetic influence from her drew them literally toward her.

Marianne heard Nat laugh softly beside her.

"Good Lord, you have to hand it to her, don't you?" he murmured. "She's got everything."

Marianne tried to find a suitable reply to that, and failed. And at that moment applause broke out around them. Lisette's was the first gown to draw applause, and although she did not actually smile, the tribute brought an expression of feline contentment to her face. But she kept her green eyes demurely lowered, until she came abreast of Nat. Then, as though she knew by instinct where he was sitting, she swept up her long lashes and smiled faintly at him.

Marianne was almost sure she heard him gasp slightly as Lisette passed on.

It was a performance that was to be repeated half a dozen times during the ensuing hour, and each time Marianne felt her nerves and her self-control stretched to breaking point.

If Nat had remained either amused or indifferent, it would not have mattered. But she knew, as clearly as if he had told her so, that Lisette got under his skin every time she batted her ridiculously long eyelashes and looked at him with those cool green eyes.

I mustn't say anything, Marianne kept on telling herself. *She's trying to provoke me, as well as stir him.*

She'd like me to put myself in the wrong with some catty remark about her. But I won't, I won't, I won't!

And at that moment Nat grinned thoughtfully and said, "Lisette certainly makes all the other girls look ordinary. It must be tough having her around."

"Were you including me in that general bit of commiseration?" asked Marianne. And she tried so hard to make that sound unworried that she succeeded in making it sound cold.

"Good heavens, no!" He sounded genuinely astonished. "I would never think of you and Lisette in the same category."

And she spent the rest of the time wondering exactly what he meant by that.

She was disappointed later to find that he was committed to seeing Lisette home. But as least he was perfectly frank about it this time.

"I'm sorry, Marianne, dear. I made the arrangement before I knew that you and I were going to meet here and make up," he said with an endearingly rueful smile. "But I'll call you up in the next day or two, and we'll go out and celebrate in a big way."

There was nothing to do but to assure him that she would be perfectly all right and that—as indeed was the case—she was sharing a taxi home with Marcelle.

Late though it was—or, rather, early now—Marcelle was still chattering happily about the events of the evening.

"In spite of the terrible incident of the brooch, it has been wonderful," she said to Marianne, balancing several purchases on her knee, while she grasped her bag with her free hand. "I have been able to buy several things for *maman*, and so she will not mind so much that I had to leave her for the evening. In this Monsieur Florian has been very kind."

"Yes, he can be kind," agreed Marianne abstractedly.

"Of course, when he is angry he is very frightening," Marcelle prattled on happily, "but then it is wonderful how she subdues him. He must love her very much."

"Yes, I suppose he does."

"It must be beautiful to be loved like that." Marcelle sighed sentimentally. "Is that how your fiancé loves you?"

"I don't know," said Marianne, rather startled by the direct question. "And, anyway, he isn't my fiancé—yet."

"But it is the young man with the romantic eyes, who sat and held your hand during the dress show, isn't it?" Marcelle pressed.

Marianne laughed protestingly.

"I don't know that he'd choose to be described that way," she said. "And anyway—it's unlucky to take too much for granted, Marcelle. Is this where you live?" she added, as the taxi drew up in a quiet street.

"Oh, yes." Marcelle tried to gather all her things together and succeeded in dropping her bag, which Marianne picked up for her.

"Shall I come and open the door for you?" Marianne volunteered.

"If you would, that would be kind. The key is in my bag. In the little pocket at the back."

"Inside the bag, you mean?" inquired Marianne, as she opened the bag and stepped out of the taxi after Marcelle.

"No, no—at the back. *Not* inside," Marcelle said over her shoulder.

But Marianne hardly heard what she said. She was staring down into Marcelle's slightly shabby little handbag. For at the bottom, winking and glittering in the light from the nearby street lamp, lay Gabrielle Florian's rose spray brooch.

CHAPTER SEVEN

"Marcelle," said Marianne, in a queer, stifled sort of voice, "do you know what you have in your handbag?"

"In my handbag?" Marcelle turned and looked at her over the parcels. "But of course. My purse, my key, my—What is it?" Suddenly her tone changed and a note of alarm was sounded. "Why do you ask that question? And why do you speak so—so queerly?"

"Because," Marianne said slowly, "you have something very odd in your handbag, Marcelle. You have Madame Florian's missing brooch."

"*I* have? Oh, no! That's impossible!" The other girl's horror was so patent that there was no doubting its reality. "In my handbag Madame Florian's brooch? Let me see."

She leaned forward, dropping two of her more awkwardly shaped parcels as she did so, and gazed into the bag. Then, at the sight of the sinister glitter, she gave a gasp and burst into tears.

"I know nothing about it," she exclaimed rapidly. "It has nothing to do with me. They will say that I stole it, but this is not true. I never stole anything in my life and I wouldn't dare to start with Madame Florian's brooch. But they will not believe me. They will say I am a thief and they will send me to prison and *maman* will die of shame."

"Nonsense," declared Marianne, who privately thought *maman* was much too tough for that. "No one's going to call you a thief while I'm around. Stop crying, Marcelle. We're going to need all our wits for this." And stooping down, she picked up the two dropped parcels.

"But what shall I do?" The actual sobs had ceased, but the frightened tears still trickled down Marcelle's cheeks.

"I'll think of something," promised Marianne, spurred to some form of reassurance by Marcelle's piteous appearance. "Can I come in with you, or is it too late?"

"No, no. It's not too late. But we must not tell *maman*," Marcelle explained quickly.

"Won't she be asleep in bed, anyway?" asked Marianne, who felt she had never liked the sound of *maman* less.

"In bed, but not asleep," Marcelle said knowledgeably.

"Oh, I see. Well—" Marianne glanced over her shoulder "—I'd better go and pay the taxi driver." By the time she returned, the door stood open and Marcelle already had a dim light on in the tiny entrance hall of the apartment.

"Marcelle..." called a fretful voice from one of the three rooms that led off the small hall.

"*Oui, maman—je viens, je viens.*" Hastily Marcelle gestured to Marianne to go into one of the other rooms. Then, quickly removing the traces of tears from her face, she went into her mother's room.

Marianne, meanwhile, entered the small, shabby, but attractive sitting room—obviously the room of people who had very little money, but a room where someone had made the very best of things, with some taste and much care.

Poor little soul, thought Marianne compassionately. *She hasn't much of a life. I must see she doesn't suffer over this wretched business. But oh, dear—I hope she won't be long!*

She sat down, stifled an involuntary yawn, and waited with what patience she could until Marcelle should have pacified *maman*. It seemed to her that the small ornate clock on the mantelpiece was ticking away almost all that was left of her precious sleeping hours, and she found herself wondering dazedly if she was ever going to get to bed that night—or rather, that morning.

At last, however, Marcelle came in, still wearing the false smile of reassurance assumed for *maman's* benefit, like a mask that she had forgotten to take off. Then she closed the door and dropped into a chair near Marianne, her pale young face suddenly drawn and scared again.

"I explained to *maman* that you were my colleague and that you had had nothing to eat or drink all the evening because we were so busy. I said you had just come in for a biscuit and a glass of wine and that we should not be more than ten minutes, so at least we have a little while to talk. Will you have a glass of wine, Marianne?" She half rose from her chair in a weary but willing way that went to Marianne's heart.

"No, no, dear. Sit still. Let's use our time for discussing this extraordinary business."

Marcelle made a helpless little gesture with her hands.

"I don't understand it at all." Again there was that dangerous quiver in her voice. "I don't understand how it could have happened, and I don't understand what on earth I am to do."

"Well, let's take things in their proper order." Marianne spoke with a firmness that was steadying in itself. "First, how could it possibly have happened? Only by accident or because someone deliberately put it there."

"Someone—not me, you mean?" Marcelle said timidly.

"Of course. I know you didn't put it there," Marianne declared in a matter-of-fact tone.

"D-do you?" Marcelle's pale face brightened a little. "How do you know?"

"First because I know you're honest. Second because I know you haven't the nerve to carry through a bold theft. And thirdly because, if you'd really taken the brooch, you would never have asked me to look for your key in your handbag. You couldn't have *forgotten* the brooch was there, if you'd taken it. It would be the thing you would be aware of above everything else. If you'd stolen the brooch and had it laying in the bottom of your handbag, you'd have dropped every one of your parcels rather than let me get my hands on the bag."

"Well—yes. I suppose you're right." A faint look of relief began to dawn on the other girl's face.

"That means that it must have got there accidentally, or by someone else's intention. Could it possibly have got there by accident?"

"How?" inquired Marcelle stupidly, and Marianne saw that, in spite of everything, she was nearly dead with sleep.

"Well—I don't know. Was the bag open at any time? Was it anywhere near the stand? Could the brooch, by any stretch of possibility, have fallen into it?"

"No, of course not," said Marcelle quite simply. "My bag was behind the stall, just as yours was. The brooch was in the very front of the stand."

"True. I didn't think it could have been an accident anyway, of course. I just wanted to—to eliminate the idea entirely," Marianne admitted. "Then there's only one other explanation, Marcelle. Someone took the brooch deliberately and just as deliberately put it in your handbag."

"But why should they?" Marcelle looked utterly bewildered. "If they wished to steal Madame Florian's brooch, why not take it away with them at once? Why give it to me?"

Marianne looked at her curiously.

"Does anyone dislike you very much, Marcelle?"

The other girl shook her head slowly.

"Why should they?" she said again. "I do not quarrel with people, and I have nothing that anyone could envy."

All too true, thought Marianne compassionately.

"Then—was it something to do with the bag itself?" She gazed thoughtfully at the offending bag as it stood upon the table, but there seemed nothing remarkable about it.

"It's quite like hundreds of other bags," Marcelle pointed out. "Intrinsically good, because it came originally from the boutique. But—black, medium-sized, inconspicuous. Rather like the one that you yourself have." She gestured vaguely toward Marianne's own handbag, and Marianne's gaze automatically followed hers.

At the same moment a curious, premonitory little chill slid down her spine.

"Marcelle...Marcelle..." called the plaintive voice from the next room, and Marcelle nervously jumped to her feet and hurried from the room.

Left alone, Marianne stared in a sort of fascination from one handbag to the other. They were not by any means identical, but they were superficially alike. Quite sufficiently alike for anyone in a hurry to mistake one for the other.

"It wasn't meant for Marcelle at all," she said in a whisper. "It was meant for *me*. And it was put there by someone who hated me enough to want to do me real harm. What was it Marcelle said? That she doesn't quarrel with people and she has nothing anyone could envy. That does apply to her, but—it isn't quite true of me."

In spite of her efforts to be just and objective, a very clear picture of Lisette, smiling secretly, rose before her.

It's absurd, Marianne tried to tell herself. *I'm becoming obsessed with the thought of her. But she hates me, and I suppose she may well envy me my friendship and reconciliation with Nat. Though, of course, the reconciliation came after the theft—or did she know that Nat and I were going to make up?*

As clearly as her weary brain would permit, Marianne reviewed the events of the evening again, and suddenly her hand went to her lips in a sort of dismayed gesture of realization.

Why, of course! She had been talking eagerly to Nat at the very moment when the brooch must have been removed. If they had not indulged in a lengthy reconciliation, at least it must have been obvious that they were exchanging rapid, eager explanations about something.

It couldn't be... Marianne thought. *And yet, what else?*

At that moment Marcelle came back into the room.

"*Maman* says our voices disturb her," she explained in an apologetic whisper, though Marianne felt sure that their voices could not have reached *maman* though the closed door. "I am sorry, Marianne, but in a few minutes you must go. *Maman's* nerves are so bad, you know, and the slightest thing upsets her."

"Yes, of course." Marianne rose automatically to her feet.

"But still we have discovered nothing about the brooch," Marcelle said despairingly.

"Yes, we have." Instinctively, Marianne too had now dropped her voice to a whisper, in deference to *maman's* nerves. "I've been thinking. That wasn't meant for your bag at all, Marcelle. It was meant for mine. Someone—whoever did it—mistook your bag for mine."

"You mean—" Marcelle's expression turned to one of incredulous hope and relief "—that the brooch should be in your bag and not in mine at all?"

"Well, yes. I suppose one might say that," agreed Marianne, who had not seen the situation in quite such compromising terms.

"But then—in that case—" Marcelle reached for the offending handbag and actually began to scrabble about among its contents for the fatal brooch "—in that case—" she produced the brooch, which lay glinting and winking provocatively in the palm of her outstretched hand "—will you—will you perhaps take it?"

"I—hadn't thought of doing that." Marianne looked taken aback.

"What had you thought of doing, then?" Marcelle watched her anxiously.

"I don't know," Marianne confessed. "It was only that I thought—I felt almost sure—that Lisette put the brooch into what she believed to be my handbag, so as to get me into trouble."

"Lisette?" In spite of *maman*, nursing her nerves in the next room, Marcelle allowed her voice to rise to an astonished squeak. "You think Lisette stole the brooch?"

"Well, she hates me. She—she has designs on someone who—who means a lot to me," Marianne explained rapidly. "I think, on the spur of the moment, she whisked the brooch away and slipped it, as she believed, into my handbag."

"But she knew you would find it when you got home."

"I think perhaps she hoped there would be a scene as soon as its loss was discovered, and that perhaps the police would be called and I would be branded as a thief right away."

"*I* would have been, you mean!" Marcelle went pale at the very thought.

"Well, yes, as it turned out, you would have been sus-pected," Marianne admitted. "But thanks to Madame Florian's angelic behavior, the whole thing was glossed over for the time being."

"I *said* Madame Florian was an angel," exclaimed Marcelle fervently. "She saved me from prison and *maman* from disgrace."

"At least she saved you from a nasty ten minutes of explanation," agreed Marianne, who stopped short of Marcelle's flights of fancy. "But we're left with the brooch. And the explanations," she added thoughtful-ly.

"To whom shall we explain?" quavered Marcelle doubtfully. "Not to the police?"

"No, no, of course not. They don't enter into it."

"To Monsieur Florian?" Marcelle looked nearly as frightened at this prospect as at the thought of the police.

"I, suppose so, yes." Marianne, too, found herself quailing a little at the thought of trying to tell their fan-tastic story to Monsieur Florian. Particularly if he should turn that icy, speculative glance upon one. Until that evening she had not been really frightened of him. But she shivered slightly, even now, as she thought of the way he had looked when he said quietly, "Tell me what happened, *mademoiselle*."

"You, too, are frightened," Marcelle said quickly. "You would not stand by me. You could not look Monsieur Florian in the face and expect him to believe that someone else stole the brooch and put it into my bag, thinking it was your bag. The story is too silly. Too— too improbable. And Monsieur Florian does not believe the improbable. He tears it to pieces and says in that cold voice of his, 'That is a lie.' ''

And to Marianne's intense dismay, Marcelle started to cry again.

"Oh, Marcelle, please...." She would have been cross if she had not realized that the other girl's nerves were worn to a thread by the miserable life she lived with her selfish, demanding mother. "Please, dear, don't cry. It won't help a bit. And of *course* I'll stand by you. In fact—all right, you'd better give me the brooch, if the very look of it makes you panic."

"You—you mean it?" Timidly, incredulously, Marcelle held out the lovely, dangerous thing once more, and with a sense of misgiving that she sternly repressed, Marianne took it and put it in her own handbag.

"Oh, Marianne, you are so good and kind. And so strong," Marcelle said enviously. "You are brave and you do not cry, and you carry any troubles so lightly. But then, of course, you have only yourself to think about. You have no *maman* to consider."

"Well—" for a moment, and with intense nostalgia, Marianne thought of her dear, commonsense, reliable parent, home in England "—I have a *maman*, but she doesn't come into the—the same category as yours, I guess. Perhaps it makes a difference."

"Oh, it does!" declared Marcelle fervently. "But what are you now going to do, Marianne. T-tell Monsieur Florian?"

"No," said Marianne, on a sudden note of inspiration. "I shall tell Madame Florian. By telephone, to-morrow morning. Or rather, later this morning."

"Madame Florian? Marianne—" the other girl gazed at her admiringly "—it is an idea of genius!"

"Well, at least she will listen more patiently, and understand more easily, than Monsieur Florian," Marianne said. "I will tell her exactly what has happened, and ask if she would like me to bring the brooch to her house, or whether she herself will fetch it from the boutique. And I will explain that I would find it a little difficult to tell our story to Monsieur Florian—and I think she will understand.''

"Of course she will understand! If she has lived with him for nearly five years, she cannot fail to understand," declared Marcelle cryptically. "And then she can explain to Monsieur Florian for us."

"Y-yes." Marianne hoped it was all going to work out as simply as it sounded at the moment. But, at any rate, Marcelle now looked as though she might manage to sleep for the few hours remaining to them.

She accompanied Marianne to the door, repeating her thanks in an emotional whisper. And Marianne, still terribly aware of her own happy, independent lot compared to that of the other girl, actually dropped a light kiss on Marcelle's cheek before she went out into the chilly Paris dawn.

Fortunately, it was a very short walk to her own place. So short that she thought sleepily, *I must manage to see something of Marcelle. It shouldn't be difficult, and the poor little thing certainly needs friends. I didn't realize she was so near.*

The last effort of climbing the stairs to her attic seemed almost unbearable, and once she stumbled and hoped guiltily that she had not disturbed anyone. But at last she was safely in her own room, and nothing else mattered but the delicious thought of sinking into bed. Not the thought of Lisette. Not the presence of Madame Florian's brooch in her bag. Not even the reconciliation with Nat.

All that she wanted was sleep—sleep—sleep. And, as her eyes finally closed, she was aware of a vague thankfulness that *she* did not have to listen for a querulous voice summoning her from the next room.

She was, however, still subject to the tyranny of her alarm clock. And a few hours later it roused her ruthlessly from a lovely dream in which she was drifting lazily along a sunlit river in a punt, while someone—she was

not quite sure if it was Nat or Roger Senloe—wielded
the pole with impressive skill.

"Oh, be *quiet!*" she admonished her shrill little
clock, and groped sleepily for it, to stop its insistent
clamor. However, she only succeeded in pushing it onto
the floor, where it continued to ring with undiminished
vigor, and so she really had to rouse herself and realize
it was another day.

Marianne was still less than half-awake, and she was
almost dressed before she fully recalled the events of the
previous evening. Half doubting her own senses, she
looked into her handbag, to make quite sure she had not
dreamed it all. For the scene in Marcelle's apartment
now seemed nearly as dim and fantastic as the scene in
the punt.

But the almost inimical sparkle of the unlucky brooch
left her no room for wishful doubting. And soberly
completing her dressing, she sat down to drink the hot
coffee and eat the rolls that were brought to her room
every morning.

In the full light of day, her suggestion about telephoning Gabrielle Florian seemed rather less of an inspiration and more of an imposition. The obvious course was
to go to her employer with her story.

But—perhaps because of the short night and the
series of shocks during the last few hours—she seemed
to have very little to the strength and courage that
Marcelle had confidently attributed to her. The idea of
facing Florian himself was, at the moment, quite simply
beyond her.

*I don't know really why I took on the whole un-
pleasant business of explaining. The wretched thing was
in Marcelle's bag, after all,* she thought crossly.

But the next minute she remorsefully admitted to herself that she knew quite well why she had done it. She
was ten times better equipped than the other girl to deal
with a crisis. And anyway, she reminded herself brac-
ingly, there was nothing particularly terrifying in
telephoning the charming Madame Florian.

She wished she could have done so right away, before

going to work. But it was obviously too early to disturb someone who had also been up until the small hours of the morning. She would have to find a suitable moment during the morning, and telephone from the booth just outside the boutique. All she could do at the moment was look up the Florians' private number and make a note of it.

Having done at least this much toward settling the whole affair, Marianne set out for work in a rather better mood.

At the boutique she found everyone somewhat inclined to relax and gossip, at least during the early part of the day before business became brisk. Even Madame Rachel, looking impeccably well groomed and soignée in spite of her short night, was in an indulgent mood. Though to Marianne she was a trifle reserved, presumably because she could not quite bring herself to overlook the unfortunate incident of the lost brooch.

If she knew I had it in my bag at this moment, she'd have a fit, thought Marianne. And for the first time it was brought home to her that she had put herself in a decidedly false position, and she longed for the time when she could rid herself of the incriminating piece of evidence.

Of Marcelle, surprisingly, there was no sign. And presently Madame Rachel, after being summoned to the telephone, came back to say that she would not be coming in to the boutique that day.

"Her mother is ill, it seems, and she cannot leave her." Madame Rachel shrugged. "She has not an easy time, that little one. Today one can be a trifle indulgent, since she worked so late last night. But it would not be good for her work if *maman* were to keep her at home too often."

Marianne felt unwarrantably depressed at Marcelle's nonappearance. Not that she was likely to be a powerful support in any moment of crisis. But at least it would have been pleasant and reassuring to be able to whisper to someone the gist of whatever conversation she had with Madame Florian. To have no one near who, even in the remotest degree, shared her anxiety made her feel unpleasantly isolated.

How strange that it isn't enough to know one is inno-cent, she reflected uncomfortably. And when Florian presently passed through the boutique on his way up to the salon, she avoided his glance and actually felt her heart beat apprehensively as though she had indeed committed some sort of crime.

But at least his presence meant that she could now safely telephone his home. And as soon as there was a lull she asked Madame Rachel if she might go and make an urgent personal telephone call.

Madame Rachel was lenient about these things, and even though Marianne was not in her good graces at this moment, she gave permission, only adding on principle, "Do not stay to gossip."

"No, *madame*," Marianne promised. And seizing her handbag, from which she now hardly dared to be parted for one instant, she made her way to the telephone booth and eagerly dialed the Florians' private number.

Almost immediately a voice that was not Gabrielle Florian's replied.

"May I speak to Madame Florian, please?" Mari-anne's voice shook a little, in spite of herself.

"*Madame* has already left for the airport," was the unexpected reply.

"The—the airport? You mean—Madame Florian has gone away?"

"*Madame* is flying to London today. Who is speak-ing, please?"

"It doesn't matter. When will she be back?"

"In a few days. Perhaps Monday—or Tuesday. Who shall I say called, please?"

"It doesn't matter," said Marianne again. And slow-ly she replaced the receiver.

A few days! One could not wait for a few days. It was impossible to take unofficial custody of stolen goods— for that was what it amounted to—for a few days. She would have to do something else.

And when she returned to the boutique and saw that

Lisette had drifted down for something, Marianne felt more than ever that she was in the falsest of false positions. Lisette was talking to Madame Rachel with that spuriously meek air that she sometimes assumed. But while she talked, her green eyes glanced around reflectively, and when they lighted on Marianne, just returned from telephoning, they looked abnormally interested.

She's wondering what I'm going to do, thought Marianne. *She's probably wondering why I haven't done anything yet. I should have spoken to Monsieur Florian as soon as he arrived. Or to Madame Rachel. I haven't done myself any good by waiting. I mean—I haven't done Marcelle any good. At least—by now I seem to be much more involved than Marcelle!*

While she was digesting this unpalatable thought, Lisette went away upstairs again.

I shall ask to see Monsieur Florian now, Marianne decided resolutely.

But before she could even speak to Madame Rachel about approaching the great man in person, the door of the boutique opened and in came Roger Senloe.

"Roger!" She was so relieved to see him that she said his name aloud, oblivious of the effect it might have on Madame Rachel, with her strict notions of proper respect to both customers and her employer's visitors.

"Hello, there." Roger smiled down at her, so reassuringly that Marianne could not imagine why she had not thought of telephoning *him* and telling *him* of her dilemma. "Recovered from the drama of last night? I hear the whole thing was an enormous financial success."

"Monsieur Florian will have the latest reports and will doubtless be happy to see you, Monsieur Senloe," Madame Rachel interposed, and she gave Marianne a quelling glance that entirely precluded any exchange of confidences.

"I'll go right up, if I may." Roger turned the full battery of his charm on the director of the boutique for a moment, in order to subdue her.

"Please do, please do." Madame Rachel was all

smiles at once. "Marianne—attend to *madame,* who wishes to see some gloves, I believe."

"Yes, *madame,*" Marianne said. But somehow—perhaps by some clever contrivance of Roger's—she was able to snatch a further word or two with him at the bottom of the stairs.

"Roger, I must see you and talk to you," she whispered urgently. "Please, please find an opportunity."

"When I come down again," he promised, also in a low voice. "Can I take you out to lunch?"

"Just coffee and a sandwich—there won't be time for more. But thank you."

And then she was at the counter, inquiring the wishes of a stout dowager, with a courteous air that really covered the most enormous relief.

It would be all right now. Roger would believe everything she said and would know how to handle the situation. Why on earth hadn't she thought of him before? But anyway, it didn't matter. She had thought of him now. And never in her life had she been more glad to remember the existence of anyone. At that moment, for her, Roger Senloe wore an outsize halo.

Her customer took a long while to decide on her purchase, but Marianne displayed admirable patience and was genuinely pleased to see her go away satisfied. Then she turned to find Madame Rachel at her elbow. And what Madame Rachel said gravely was, "You are wanted in Monsieur Florian's office, Marianne."

"In Monsieur Florian's office?" It was an unusual summons for one of the junior *vendeuses,* and Madame Rachel's expression said as much. Insensibly, Marianne's heart skipped a beat. Then she told herself, somewhat illogically, that Roger must have guessed what had happened, and that this was his way of giving her a chance to tell her story to them both.

She knew the next minute that this was impossible, of course. But, in any case, one did not keep Monsieur Florian waiting. So she smoothed her hair with a slightly unsteady hand and prepared to obey his summons.

At the last moment she caught up her handbag—but

whether because she still dared not leave it unattended
or because she believed that she could at last hand over
the brooch, she was not quite sure.

There were two flights of stairs to climb to Monsieur
Florian's office, and Marianne was slightly breathless
when she finally knocked on the door and, in answer to
his abrupt, "Come in," entered.

The famous designer was sitting behind is desk, a not
very prepossessing expression on his worn, clever face,
and Roger Senloe was sitting at the side of the desk,
looking unusually grave.

"Sit down, *mademoiselle*." Florian indicated the seat
immediately opposite himself, and it seemed to Marianne's excited fancy that his cold glance rested for a moment on the bag she was clutching.

She sat down and waited. And after a moment
Florian leaned forward, his hands clasped lightly on the
desk in front of him, and addressed her with a sort of
courteous deliberation that was curiously without reassurance.

"*Mademoiselle*," he said, "I am going to make a very
curious request of you. You may consider it an unpar-
donable request, and you are quite at liberty to refuse it.
But I hope you will not do so." He paused for a moment, though his glance did not move from her face.
"Would you be good enough to open your handbag and
show me what you have inside it?"

CHAPTER EIGHT

DON'T PANIC, Marianne told herself in what she knew was a moment of real peril, though it was hard to think of anything but Florian's cold gray eyes looking at her so uncompromisingly. Then she heard herself say quietly, "It is simpler if I tell you, *monsieur*. I have Madame Florian's brooch in my bag." She heard Roger catch his breath. "I was waiting for a suitable moment to bring it to you."

"You have had several suitable moments during the morning, *mademoiselle*," Florian said dryly. "And still more suitable moments last night. Explain yourself."

"I couldn't bring it to you last night, *monsieur*. We—I didn't find it until we—I got home."

"But you have had it with you all this morning? And you didn't bring it to me until you were summoned and challenged. Why?"

"I tried to telephone Madame Florian, *monsieur*. I thought—"

"Why Madame Florian?" His eyebrows went up.

"Because she is much less intimidating than you, *monsieur*," Marianne said with desperate truth. "She would not speak to me as you're speaking to me now, making me feel guilty when I am innocent. She would listen while I told my story—"

"I, too, am listening, and I invite you to tell your story," Florian observed dryly. But insensibly his voice was less cold, and he leaned back in his chair with a more relaxed air.

"Perhaps if I did the questioning—" Roger began.

"Thank you, *mon ami*," said Florian without even looking at him, "but I prefer to handle my own staff in my own way. Proceed, *mademoiselle*."

So *mademoiselle,* somewhat stumblingly, proceeded. As simply and briefly as possible, she told how she and Marcelle had discovered the missing brooch in Marcelle's handbag, and almost immediately Florian interrupted her.

"Then you mean—it was not in your handbag at all?" He looked surprised and, in some grim way, intrigued.

"No, *monsieur.* It was not in my handbag. But I think it was intended to be there."

"Why do you think that?"

"Because whoever planted it there wanted to get someone into serious trouble. Marcelle, as she explained to me herself, has no enemies. Nor is there any reason someone else might envy or hate her."

"A cheerless lot," commented Florian with a slight grimace. "But there is another explanation, *mademoiselle.* Have you not thought of it? If, as you say, the brooch was in Marcelle's bag, might the simple explanation not be that she stole it herself?"

"Oh, she *couldn't,*" Marianne stated with simple conviction. "She's honest, she's timid—and she invited me, for no reason but the obvious one, to look in her handbag for her latchkey. But for that suggestion of hers, I should never have seen the brooch."

"Hmm, yes—that does seem to dispose of Marcelle," Florian agreed thoughtfully. "That is, if your story is true, *mademoiselle,* and not just concocted on the spur of the moment."

"Really, Florian...." Roger shifted angrily in his seat, but a gesture from Florian silenced him again.

"Monsieur Florian," said Marianne, looking directly at him, "it is quite easy for you to prove my story. Marcelle has not come into work today because her mother is ill. I have had no way of communicating with her since last night. If you would like to telephone her now, you can confirm everything I have said."

"It is a good idea," Florian agreed calmly. And reaching for the telephone, he asked the operator to find Mademoiselle Marcelle's telephone number and put him through.

While they waited, Marianne stared at the floor. She knew instinctively that if she looked up she would draw a sympathetic glance from Roger, and she could have done with it. But she also knew that Florian wanted no personal element to be introduced into this conversation until he himself was satisfied of her innocence. And Florian's wishes were the ones that counted at the moment.

"Ah, Marcelle," she heard him say after a pause, and his tone was pleasant and unalarming. "This is Monsieur Florian—"

But evidently the mere mention of his name was enough to uncork Marcelle's rush of explanations and apologies. For three solid minutes he sat there, unable to get in more than an occasional, "So?"

Then he said firmly, "Thank you, Mademoiselle Marcelle. You have been most helpful and explicit. My compliments to your mother, and I hope she will soon be well. Please don't worry further. The brooch is in my office now and will be returned to my wife without delay. Goodbye."

As he replaced the receiver there was a glint of unmistakable amusement in his eyes. Then he smiled faintly at Marianne.

"Your story has been amply confirmed, *mademoiselle*. But I still do not see why you took on the explanations for Marcelle."

"She was afraid to make them herself, *monsieur*."

"She seemed to be under no difficulty of the sort just now," he remarked dryly.

"Oh, but that's different! You're not so—I mean—on the telephone it's much easier."

"Miss Marianne means that the very sight of you strikes terror into your employees," put in Roger, with a certain amount of enjoyment, Marianne thought.

"Am I *so* terrifying?" Florian looked at Marianne and smiled, that singularly attractive smile that he could use if he liked.

"At times, *monsieur,* yes," she said frankly, though with an apologetic little laugh. "I would not like to face you if I had really done something wrong. And I didn't relish the idea even when I *appeared* to have done something wrong. That was why it seemed so much easier to explain to Madame Florian. I did telephone her, as your maid will confirm—though I didn't leave my name," she added as an afterthought. "But I learned that *madame* had just left for the airport."

"Yes, that's true. She will be away for a few days. But if you will give me the brooch, *mademoiselle,* I shall be happy to return it to her when she comes home."

"Oh, yes of course!" Marianne opened her bag, took out the brooch and thankfully handed it to her employer. "I *am* glad to see that satisfactorily ended," she exclaimed.

"But it's not ended," cut in Roger on a grim note that Marianne had not heard in his voice before. "Somebody tried hard to make you out to be a thief, and we have to get to the bottom of that. Have you any idea who might have wanted to do this monstrous thing to you, Marianne?"

There was a moment's pause. Then Marianne said quietly, "Before I answer that or accuse anyone unjustly, will you tell me, Monsieur Florian, what—or who—gave you the idea that I had the brooch in my handbag?"

Immediately a disagreeable expression came over Florian's face, and she saw that, for his own reasons, he would very much have preferred not to stir up further trouble.

"Now that the brooch has been returned and you have been exonerated, is that not sufficient, *mademoiselle*?"

"No, it is *not* sufficient!" That was Roger Senloe again—more indignant on Marianne's behalf, it seemed, than she was herself. "Stop being so confounded disingenuous, Florian. You know perfectly well that that sly little redhead couldn't have come making insinuations if she hadn't known more about this business than she should."

"My dear Roger, I don't know how you got into the

diplomatic service—and, still less, how you stay there—
if that's your way of handling a delicate matter,"
retorted Florian with some annoyance.

"Never mind about that." Roger was suddenly cheerful again. "Miss Lisette—or whatever her name is—
isn't the kind to be dealt with in tactful memoranda.
Blunt and brutal, that's the handling for her."

Florian drummed angrily on the desk with his long
fingers and frowned, so that in an odd way Marianne
was slightly sorry for him.

"Monsieur Florian," she said, "I do understand that
you don't want trouble in the firm, but I would like to
know—was it Lisette who told you I probably had the
brooch in my handbag?"

"Yes, of course."

"Then I'm afraid she also thought she had put it
there. First of all, she counted on your calling in the
police last night, in which case we should probably have
had to turn out our bags, and I—or, as it turned out,
Marcelle—would have been in a very awkward position.
But Madame Florian's kind indulgence saved us from
that."

"That must have been a disappointment for the little
so-and-so," observed Roger savagely.

"After that, she probably hoped that I would be so
nonplussed and horrified when I discovered the thing in
my bag that I wouldn't know at first what to do. Which
was true, of course."

"On the contrary, she probably judged you by herself," said Roger uncharitably, "and decided that you
would hang onto it, since you had unwittingly got it
safely away."

"No, no—" Marianne shook her head and smiled
"—she was pretty sure I had it in my bag still, which
wouldn't have been the case if I had just decided to keep
it. I remember now—she obviously noticed that I was
reluctant to be parted from my bag, even when I just
slipped out to the telephone booth. She made a shrewd
guess at the reason, and went straight upstairs and told
you I had the brooch in my bag, I suppose?"

"She did," agreed Florian curtly.

"And you believed her immediately? Oh, Monsieur Florian!" said Marianne, a trifle reproachfully.

"I have not your beautiful faith in human nature, *mademoiselle*," replied Florian, with a dry smile. "But in point of fact, I did *not* believe her. I thought, however, that you should have a chance of clearing yourself in front of an impeccable witness—" He inclined his head inclined his head ironically in Roger's direction. "I assure you, I was both astounded and disappointed when you calmly confessed to having the brooch in your bag."

"Thank you," said Marianne with a smile, and she herself would have left things there.

Roger, however, was obstinately determined otherwise, it seemed.

"Well, now we've got to the bottom of that—and found who tried to blacken Marianne's character in this odious way—what do we do next?" he inquired briskly.

"Nothing," said Florian disagreeably.

"*Nothing?* My dear Florian, have you no regard at all for common justice?"

"Not much, if it conflicts with the interests of my collection," replied the Frenchman coolly. "Lisette is the best model I've had since I married Gabrielle and took her out of the firm."

"But the girl's a menace! She should be fired."

"So was Héloise a menace, if you remember, when she tried to get Gabrielle into trouble," observed Florian reflectively. "But I did not fire her."

"You threatened her with dismissal, if I remember rightly."

"Ah, that's different. I shall threaten Lisette with dismissal," Florian said pleasantly.

"I thought you said you were not going to do anything further," Roger objected.

"You are mistaken, *mon ami*. You asked me what *we* were going to do next. And I replied, quite truthfully, 'Nothing'. The rest is entirely in my hands and I must beg you to leave it there. Marianne will now return to the boutique. You will go about your own affairs. And I—" a reflective look came into those cold gray eyes "—I shall see Lisette."

"Oh, well—come, that's all right." Roger was almost genial, now that he felt justice was about to be done. And glancing at his watch, he got to his feet.

"When is your lunchtime, Marianne?"

"In about ten minutes' time."

"Very well. I'll wait for you outside."

"Thank you." She smiled at him and also got to her feet. Florian gave her a not unfriendly little nod of dismissal, and the interview was at an end.

Downstairs in the boutique once more, she was aware that Madame Rachel gave her one or two curious glances. But, as she was not aware how much Monsieur Florian wanted said about the whole incident, it was not possible even to tell her that Madame Florian's brooch had been found.

However, she gathered by now that Monsieur Florian had his own methods in these matters, and she guessed that in time Madame Rachel would be given a more or less satisfactory account of what had happened.

Roger came downstairs a few minutes after her, paused for a pleasant word with Madame Rachel and then went out into the street. And when Marianne emerged from the boutique five minutes later he was a little way down the street, examining the contents of a jeweler's window with apparent interest.

"Oh, Roger—" she came up to him with her eyes shining and her cheeks pink "—thank you so much! You defended my interest marvelously."

"I don't know that I did much." He grinned and tucked her arm into his in a friendly way. "I wasn't allowed to."

"Oh, you did! You said far more than I could possibly have said myself."

"Well, at least I managed to bring the subject back to the real offender. Florian really is the limit! I believe he would have let the whole thing simmer down, if he had had his way."

"Perhaps, I don't know. Anyway I'm so glad you were there." She pressed his arm with eager fingers and somehow liked the feel of the firm muscle beneath the tweed coat. "Though Florian has his own ways of doing things. I think he'll make Lisette sorry she ever started her tricks."

"I hope so," Roger said heartily. "I still think she should have been fired. But then I haven't the same tender regard for the collection that you all have. What has she got against you, anyway, Marianne? I didn't know anyone *could* hate you so much."

"Oh—she's the one who wants Nat," Marianne explained comprehensively.

"And Nat, I take it, is the man in your life?"

"Why—yes. Oh, I forgot that I never told you his name. But, now that everything looks like it will be all right, I can say more. Yes, yes, indeed Nat is the man in my life." She laughed happily. "He always has been. There've been some ups and downs, and a good deal of misunderstanding since he came to Paris—most of which I've unloaded onto you before," she added remorsefully. "But last night we had a—a—"

"Full-scale reconciliation," he suggested obligingly.

"Yes. I think one could call it that." Marianne smiled as she reviewed the evening in retrospect.

"And Lisette, judging the signs correctly, decided to remove you from the scene in another way?"

"I'm afraid that was probably it." Marianne nodded gravely at the thought of such baseness. "You wouldn't think anyone could do such a thing, would you?"

"Indeed I would," Roger assured her cheerfully. "The Lisettes of this world are capable of almost anything. They see what they want, and absolutely nothing else matters. I hope your Nat still has a tough line of defense."

"Why?" She glanced at him a little anxiously.

"There might well be further trouble. That green-eyed little cat isn't one to give up easily. Tell me—" they had been walking along arm in arm, and at this point he steered her neatly into a pleasant café ''—what is Nat's own reaction to Miss Lisette?''

Marianne avoided answering that until they were seated at a table together. And then, since Roger continued to look mildly inquiring, she said reluctantly, ''I don't think he regards her exactly as I do.''

''That would be asking rather a lot of him,'' Roger said judicially. ''Particularly if he'd started by falling for her in a big way. Did he?''

''I—don't think it was as definite as that.'' Marianne moved uneasily, because, even to herself, she had never put things quite so clearly as that. ''It's more—''

She stopped while a very trim-looking waitress came up and took Roger's order for coffee and sandwiches.

''It's more—what?'' He turned back to Marianne as soon as the girl had gone.

''Do you really want to know?'' She laughed doubtfully. ''I mean—all the details and the shades of meaning?''

''I find it absorbing,'' he assured her.

''Do other people confide in you in this way?'' Marianne asked curiously.

''Sometimes, It's the natural lot of the middle-aged bachelor who has been crossed in love.''

''Don't be absurd!'' Marianne's laugh sounded almost shocked that time. ''And you're not middle-aged.''

''I'll never see thirty-five again,'' he stated solemnly.

''Meaning, I suppose, that you're just thirty-six,'' retorted Marianne.

''Well, yes.'' He grinned.

''And do you really consider yourself—what you said?''

''Crossed in love?''

''Um-hm.''

''Undoubtedly. Since Madame Rachel has made you a present of the story, I don't see how I can deny it.''

''Oh, you're not being serious!''

''But I am serious,'' he assured her. ''Think for yourself. You saw Gabrielle last night, in her sweetest and yet firmest mood. Do you really think that anyone could be in love with her—and completely get over it?''

''Not completely, no. But—'' Marianne looked down disturbedly at the sandwiches, which had now been placed in front of her ''—do you mean that you—you wouldn't ever get over it sufficiently to want to marry someone else?''

''I never have reached that point,'' he said dryly, pouring out her coffee for her. ''But we were talking about Nat, you know.''

''Were we?''

''And his reactions to Lisette.''

She saw she must not press him further.

''Well, I can't pretend that I really *know* his reactions for certain. I think he was greatly attracted by her when he first met her—which was the dangerous time just after he and my sister had broken their engagement. I—I don't *think* he takes her very seriously.'' Marianne frowned thoughtfully. ''But, though I thought I knew him very well, I realize that I've never seen Nat with anyone of her type before. Someone with lots of what I suppose one must call allure. Does that sound rather catty?''

''Not in the least. It sounds a very good summing up. Don't be too scrupulous where Miss Lisette is concerned, or you'll find yourself pushed to the wall. I hope you're going to tell Nat the story of the brooch—in detail.''

''Oh, no! I don't think I could. It seems mean, somehow. Since it didn't succeed, I mean.''

''And a fine chance you'd have had of telling the story if it had succeeded,'' Roger reminded her bluntly. ''Of course you must tell him. It's a very revealing sort of story.''

''But it will sound so exactly like telling tales out of school,'' protested Marianne.

''Not if you tell it amusingly and with a lightly scornful touch,'' retorted Roger shrewdly. ''Tell it as though it didn't surprise you very much that she could act that way and as though you assume, since he knows her, that he won't be surprised, either—only amused and a little disgusted.''

Marianne stared at Roger in real surprise.

"You know, I hadn't thought of it before—but I believe you could be rather a dangerous person,'' she said gravely.

He laughed a good deal at that.

"You mean I'm not quite so simple as I look?''

"I didn't mean that at all,'' she replied indignantly. "I think you look frightfully intelligent and—and interesting. But—''

"No, no! Don't add or subtract anything,'' he begged, still laughing. "That's a charming statement as it stands. Have some more coffee.''

"I'm afraid not—'' she glanced at her watch ''—I must go. It's been absolutely wonderful coming out with you like this, and I feel completely cheered and confident again, after the shattering experiences of this morning.''

"But you haven't told me why you wanted to speak to me,'' he reminded her.

"Why I wanted . . . ?'' She looked puzzled.

"You remember. You told me at the bottom of the stairs that you simply had to see me about something.''

"Oh, that! It was about the brooch, of course. Before the scene in Monsieur Florian's office I just couldn't imagine what I was to do, and then he forced my hand. But I was frantic with worry at the moment when you came into the boutique. I'd just phoned Madame Florian and found she was away from home, and I didn't know what I could do. And suddenly you walked in, and I thought—why on *earth* hadn't I thought of you before? I knew everything would be all right if I could just explain it to you,'' she finished simply.

"Did you really, Marianne?'' he said quite gravely. "I'm very glad if you feel like that. I hope you always will.''

"Well, I—I don't mean that I would impose on the feeling too much . . . .'' She blushed a little. "And now I really must go.''

"If you wait a moment while I pay the bill, I'll take you back by taxi."

"No—please stay and finish your own coffee at leisure. Madame Rachel will look censorious if I appear back in your company. She thinks you're terribly exalted because you know Monsieur Florian so well, and she already feels I'm getting a bit above my boots because I call you Roger."

"Very well," he agreed, laughing. But he came to the door of the café with her, and when he took leave of her he lightly kissed her hand.

Diplomatic training, perhaps, thought Marianne as she scurried back to the boutique. But she didn't really think Roger made a practice of kissing hands, and she felt oddly flattered as well as pleased as she recalled the light touch of his lips on the back of her hand.

When she reached the boutique once more, although she was in good time and unaccompanied by Monsieur Florian's exalted friend, Madame Rachel gave her a very thoughtful glance. However, this was explained later when she came up to Marianne and said in a confidential tone, "I have heard that the brooch was found."

"Oh, *madame*—who told you?"

"Monsieur Florian, naturally. And—" she pressed her lips together "—he also told me, in confidence of course, what happened. He wished me to know that both you and Marcelle were blameless."

"Did he really? I'm very glad," said Marianne, a good deal touched by this unexpected evidence of thoughtfulness on her employer's part.

"This does not alter the fact that you should not have left your post when you did," Madame Rachel reminded her severely.

"No, *madame*," Marianne agreed remorsefully.

"But since all has now ended well, we will say no more," concluded the director of the boutique magnanimously. "One thing only I will add. Be careful of the little Lisette. She is a bad enemy."

"I'm sure she is," Marianne agreed. "But there's not much she can do now. I'm not afraid."

"Nor was Red Riding Hood before she knew the true nature of the wolf," observed Madame Rachel succinctly, which made Marianne feel oddly uncomfortable.

Fortunately she saw nothing of Lisette during the rest of that afternoon, so she was not called on to decide what her attitude should be. In fact, Madame Rachel sent her home half an hour early, telling her to make up some of the sleep she had lost the previous night. A piece of advice Marianne was only too glad to follow.

The next day was Saturday, which meant only a half day at the boutique. But it was a busy half day, for Marcelle was still away, and Marianne was not sorry when at last release came. She felt more than ready for a weekend's relaxation.

All the same, when she had had a leisurely lunch, she decided to call in and see Marcelle, in case there was anything she could do for her. Besides, she guessed that Marcelle would like some account of what had really happened with regard to the brooch.

It was a slightly worn and harassed Marcelle who greeted her. But she was obviously pleased to see Marianne and conducted her immediately into the little sitting room.

"*Maman* is really ill this time," she explained, with an unconscious emphasis on the "really" that showed that she was defeated, rather than convinced, by *maman's* usual symptoms.

"What makes you think it's real this time?" inquired Marianne curiously.

"She does not complain," Marcelle said simply, and Marianne felt there was nothing to add to that. So, after a moment's pause, she launched into an account of her interview with Florian, while Marcelle contributed exclamations and occasional questions, but otherwise hung on every word.

"Monsieur Senloe is a good friend," she said in the end.

"Yes, indeed. But Monsieur Florian was quite a

sport, too," Marianne conceded. "I'm glad he saw fit to clear us, so far as Madame Rachel was concerned. But I *would* like to know what he really said to Lisette."

"She will hate us both now," said Marcelle worriedly.

"So what?" replied Marianne with a shrug.

"I do not like to be hated. It makes me nervous," Marcelle explained.

"I don't know that I like it particularly," Marianne admitted. "But sometimes it can't be helped. Anyway, there's nothing much she can do now. Can I help you in any way, Marcelle? Do some shopping for you or something?"

"Thank you, but no. The *femme de chambre* has been and she had done the shopping. You go home and rest now," Marcelle said. "But it is nice to know that you are near."

"Well, if you want me, you know where to find me." Marianne repeated her address. "Don't mind asking me, Marcelle, if there is anything I can do."

And she was pleased to see that Marcelle looked happier and less forlorn when she went away.

Marianne walked slowly back to her own lodging, trying to decide whether she would really rest or try to telephone Nat. He might well be busy on some assignment, she knew. But if he were free....

With a smile, she thought of the way he had held her hand as they watched the dress show, and how relieved he, too, had been to find that they were friends again. Perhaps Roger was right, and she *should* tell him some version of the brooch incident. If only for his own good, maybe he should have a better understanding of Lisette's real character. Or was that just being catty?

Before she had decided this interesting point, she arrived at her home, and the question of what she should do was immediately solved for her by the fact that Nat's familiar car was standing outside the house. He himself was sitting at the wheel reading a newspaper, with an air of having been there some time.

"Why, Nat—" She came up and addressed him

through the open window "—are you waiting for me? I didn't think—"

"Yes, I am," he said. And he dropped the newspaper and looked at her, but quite unsmilingly. "Would you get in, Marianne?" He leaned over and opened the door for her. "I'd like to talk to you."

"Well—of course." She got into the car and sat down. "But I'm not late for an appointment or anything, am I? We didn't *make* any appointment. Is there anything wrong, Nat?"

"Yes, there is," he replied dryly. "I'd like to know why you've done this cruel and shocking thing to Lisette."

CHAPTER NINE

"I? I'M SUPPOSED to have done a cruel and shocking thing to Lisette?" Marianne's voice shook slightly with indignation. "I like that! She nearly got me into the most appalling trouble, and it's no thanks to her that I'm not facing a nasty police inquiry at this moment."

"Marianne, really! How can you take this exaggerated and unreasonable view of an unfortunate mistake? Granted she didn't act in a particularly friendly manner, but you really did take a sledgehammer to crush a fly. Do you know that Lisette is in danger of losing her job because of you?"

"Serves her right!" ejaculated Marianne, understandably if unwisely.

"Good Lord, you girls are hard when you really get up against each other," exclaimed Nat disgustedly.

"No worse than you men," retorted Marianne with spirit. "Though, to tell the truth, I don't actually wish Lisette out of a job. Except that I suppose she could get another one at a rival fashion house without difficulty, which would be much more comfortable for me," she added thoughtfully.

"Is that all you have to say about it?" inquired Nat coldly.

"Well, no." Marianne turned and looked at him. "But it was you who started the subject, Nat. Maybe it's you who should say some more. I'd like to know what sort of story Lisette has told you, for one thing."

"The truth, I imagine," replied Nat dryly.

"I don't imagine anything of the kind," retorted Marianne, but quite good-humoredly. "Anyway, I'd like to hear."

"I don't know quite what you want to hear." Nat

spoke stiffly. "It was obvious from your first reply that you knew what I was referring to."

"But not the terms in which you had heard the story, Nat. I think you should tell me," said Marianne more quietly. "There seems a—a discrepancy somewhere."

"Well, as you must know perfectly well, Lisette thought she saw Madame Florian's missing brooch in your handbag.

"How?" inquired Marianne crisply.

"I don't know. Presumably she saw the thing sparkling when you opened the bag or something of the sort. In any case, as I understand it, you did have the brooch in your bag. That bit isn't in question, is it?"

"No. It's true the brooch was there, though Lisette had no opportunity whatever of seeing it, I might say. But go on."

"Well, again as you know, she went to Florian and told him she knew where the missing brooch was. I'm not going to say it was a particularly nice or high-minded thing to do—"

"No, indeed!"

"And I understand your being a bit sore about things. But appearances were certainly against you, Marianne, and it's not unreasonable that Lisette should jump to the conclusion that you had pinched the brooch since unquestionably it was in your bag. I suppose the obvious thing *was* to go to her employer about it. Particularly as the thing belonged to his wife."

"She could have spoken to me about it, too, couldn't she?" said Marianne dryly.

"The answer to that is—why should she?" retorted Nat. "You and she are not exactly friendly, are you?"

"No," said Marianne, without elaboration.

"Well, there you are. She did what most people would have done in the circumstances, I suppose. And, considering you were able to explain the whole thing to Florian and were not involved in any trouble, I think it was pretty mean of you to start making suggestions that she had herself planted the brooch in your bag and tried to get you branded as a thief. It's unworthy of you, Marianne, to invent a story of that sort!''

"Unfortunately, I didn't invent any story," Marianne replied dryly. "That bit happens to be true."

"You have no proof whatever."

"There is such a strong presumption of truth that neither Monsieur Florian nor Roger Senloe—''

"Oh, so he's in it, too, is he?" Nat looked disgusted.

"What do you mean by 'in it, too'?" demanded Marianne, suddenly really angry. "He happened to be there when Florian questioned me, and jolly glad I was of his support, too."

"He's the chap for whom you turned me down the other night, isn't he?" inquired Nat irrelevantly.

"No, he's not. He's the chap I refused to turn down for you the other night," retorted Marianne crisply. "If you remember, it was he who got in first with his invitation."

"Well, anyway, you went out with him when I wished you'd come with me. Don't expect me to admire his blue eyes in consequence." And for a moment a welcome smile flitted over Nat's face, as though he had recovered a glimmer of his usual sense of humor.

"Oh, Nat—" she melted immediately "—what on earth are we quarreling about? You don't have to like Roger if you don't want to, though he's a darling, really. And, incidentally, his eyes are gray. But that's beside the point. The real trouble is this miserable business about Lisette. I'm afraid she *did* put the wretched brooch in my bag. Or, rather, she put it in Marcelle's by mistake—''

"How do you know it was Lisette?" Nat reiterated obstinately.

"Because someone *must* have put it there. It couldn't have got there by accident, and—''

"Why does it have to be Lisette?" Nat's voice was cold and unfriendly again.

"Because, Nat, only the person who put the brooch in Marcelle's bag, thinking it was mine, could then confidently make the statement that she thought I had the brooch in my bag."

"But I've told you, she thought she saw the brooch in your bag during the morning."

"And *I* have told *you*," Marianne repeated patiently, "that she quite simply couldn't have done so."

"Oh, really—this is where we came in!" exclaimed Nat impatiently. "You prefer to reject the perfectly obvious explanation in favor of the story you cooked up from Florian, in order to get Lisette into trouble because you don't like her."

"Nat, you don't really think that's the way I behave, do you?" Marianne said quietly. "You've known me well—for quite a long time now. Is that as far as you've got with understanding me and my natural reactions?"

"Well—" he looked taken aback and slightly ashamed "—it isn't like you in the ordinary way, I know. That's why I got so mad at the thought of it. But you're jealous of Lisette, aren't you? And—"

"How dare you say that!" Marianne interrupted coldly. "Why should I be jealous of her?"

"Oh, hang it, Marianne—" he looked profoundly uncomfortable for a moment "—I didn't mean to put it as crudely as that. You don't like her, let's say. And so you simply won't admit that she might well have had a glimpse of the inside of your bag. You prefer the complicated story that makes her out to be an absolute outsider."

"Since you've used the word," said Marianne, unwisely abandoning her self-control at that moment, "that is exactly what she is. There was no possible chance of her seeing inside my bag yesterday morning, for the simple reason that I thought of little else but keeping it away from observation. If you're walking around with stolen goods in your handbag, you don't go clicking it open and shut when anyone else is around. She based her statement to Florian on the belief that she had put the brooch in my bag the previous evening. And because she saw me clutching it with exaggerated care, she guessed I'd still got the thing with me. It was a plant, and a particularly spiteful and malicious plant. And that, if you want to know, is exactly typical of your little redheaded friend.''

There was a slight silence, during which Marianne had time to recollect that, however well reasoned one's statements may be, it is always poor policy to run down another girl to a man who likes her a little too well.

"Is that all you want to say?" asked Nat, at last.

"Isn't it enough?" She gave a half angry and half contrite little laugh.

"More than enough."

"Do you want to make any comment?"

"No."

"Then. . . ." She hesitated. And then it was borne in on her, with a sense of shock, that he was simply waiting for her to get out of his car.

"Nat," she said beseechingly, "don't you see that there's no room for error? Either she or I must be telling a deliberate lie. You've only got to decide, from your knowledge of both of us, which that is likely to be."

"I don't want to discuss it any more."

"You mean that you accept Lisette's version?"

"I mean that I know you're not telling me a deliberate lie, Marianne. It simply isn't in you to do such a thing. But I think you've been uncommonly hard and prejudiced about this, and you've let that cloud your judgment. In consequence, Lisette is likely to lose her wonderful job for a comparatively small offense."

Marianne bit her lip very hard, to keep herself from breaking out into furious argument. And, after a moment, she was able to say coldly. "Lisette is not going to lose her job, if that's what is really upsetting you."

"Florian has told her that he will think it over during the weekend, but that he rather doubts if he will keep her on."

Good old Florian, thought Marianne, and had great difficulty in not saying it. As it was, she managed to say in a composed sort of way, "I doubt if he will really want to part with his best model."

"I hope you're right," replied Nat dryly. And then,

incredibly, she realized that the interview was at an end. There was nothing to do but get out of the car with what dignity she could muster, and bid him a somewhat stiff goodbye through the window.

"Goodbye," replied Nat, without any qualification, and drove away.

Marianne turned and went slowly into the house, divided between anger and an unspeakable depression, which grew heavier with every step as she ascended to her attic. Now, of course, she could think of several infinitely better ways in which she could have conducted that conversation. But alas, the chance was gone.

It was mad of me to show my real opinion of Lisette so clearly, she thought dejectedly. *However mulishly stupid he was about her. I should somehow have remained cool and objective. But when people start telling you black's white, and that you're the offender instead of the victim, it isn't possible to remain calm. I could hit him even now, when I think of it!*

The fresh surge of anger served to sustain her spirits for a short while. But then down they went again, at the reflection that she had parted from Nat in coldness and anger, and that any prospect of seeing him again in the very near future simply did not exist.

She had enjoyed the doubtful satisfaction of speaking her mind about Lisette. But the price had been her renewed friendship with Nat.

"Sometimes one *has* to say the truth!" she muttered resentfully. "I was perfectly justified in saying what I did."

But to be justified in one's utterance and to be wise in it are two entirely different things, as Marianne knew all too well. And she spent a wretched evening digesting the fact that she had only confirmed Nat's belief in Lisette's touching innocence, and wondering just how cleverly Lisette was now exploiting that fact.

If Nat was in the mood to have his sympathies played upon, Lisette was the girl to do it.

The trouble is that I'm not half as clever as she is,

thought Marianne grimly. *She outmaneuvers me every time.*

She would have spent a miserable Sunday, too, if her friendly American neighbor, Sadie, had not come knocking on her door early in the afternoon.

"I can't offer you anything as gorgeous as the ticket you got me for the Charities Fair," she explained. "But I do have two tickets for the new film at the Oubliette. Come and have something to eat with me early this evening and we'll go on to the show together if you've nothing better to do."

Marianne was only too grateful for the distraction. And later, over a modest but pleasant little meal, when Sadie asked her for *her* account of what happened at the Charities Fair, she found herself recounting the story of the stolen brooch and its eventual recovery in Marcelle's bag.

"But how turrible!" cried Sadie, becoming more Middle West than usual in her excitement. "And to think that no one guessed what a drama was in progress. Just wait till I write home to my family with this story. They'll really believe I'm seeing life."

"Rather an uncomfortable slice of life for those concerned," Marianne assured her. But she laughed and prepared to tell the rest of the tale, for Sadie was one of the world's great listeners. She could remain silent for long periods, but with her whole attention concentrated in her expressive face, and from time to time she emitted just those ejaculations and questions that give fresh impetus to a flagging tale.

She seemed to realize by instinct just why it was disastrous that Lisette should capture Nat's sympathies while Marianne was labeled in his mind as the stony-hearted aggressor. And, at the conclusion of the story she burst out with Marianne's own inevitable conclusion, "She outsmarted you, honey. Your Nat likes the picture of this Lisette as a poor little victim, so he's got to find a persecutor for her. And that's you."

"I know. But just tell me how we're going to reverse the roles now," said Marianne with a sigh.

"You can't," stated Sadie with finality. "He's never seen you in a pathetic light and he's not going to start now. He thinks you direct events. He can't see you being overtaken by them. You must take another line entirely. I think you're going to have to be big and noble about this."

"I don't want to be big and noble," retorted Marianne rather crossly. "And anyway, how can I?"

Sadie stirred her coffee thoughtfully.

"He thinks you're responsible for getting Lisette into undeserved trouble, doesn't he?"

"Yes."

"Well, then, you've got to be responsible for getting her *out* of the trouble," Sadie declared with an air of decision.

"You think so?" Marianne looked doubtful. "But—how?"

"You'll have to go to Monsieur Florian—my, how I envy you for knowing that fascinating creature—and plead Lisette's cause and say you don't want her fired on your account."

"But I don't think he's going to fire her, anyway," objected Marianne.

"*She* does, though," Sadie pointed out shrewdly. "Tell him...." She paused and looked thoughtfully at Marianne. "Can you put all the cards on the table, so far as Florian is concerned?"

"How do you mean?"

"Can you tell him that Lisette is making trouble with your boyfriend, by appearing to be the victim of your ill nature?"

"I don't know. It depends a lot on the mood he's in," Marianne said slowly. "There are times when you would hardly dare to say good morning to Florian. And at others it's all you can do not to tell him your life history and your inmost thoughts."

Sadie laughed a good deal at that.

"Well, try to catch him in the right mood," she said, "and ask him to reinstate Lisette and to let her know that it's because of *you* that he's doing it. Could you ask that?"

"I—I might. But I don't know that it would cut much ice with Lisette, even if he did tell her that."

"If she's been genuinely afraid of being fired, it won't be without effect."

"N-no. That's true. But I can't see her telling Nat."

"*You* must do that," Sadie pointed out. "You call him up and say you've interceded with Florian and that Lisette won't be fired after all. And I'm afraid—if you think he's worth it—you'd better take a good mouthful of humble pie and say it was because of what he said that you felt you should do something to help Lisette. After that he'll be ready to reopen the subject in a much better mood, and you can unsay some of the unwise things you did say, and add some noble comments that leave Lisette looking less of a victim and more of a menace."

"It's—an idea. . . ." Marianne laughed doubtfully.

"At least it gives you a chance of contacting your Nat, instead of leaving the field free for her," Sadie commented shrewdly.

"I'll think it over," Marianne promised. And she thought it over to such good purpose that she hardly followed the thread of the excellent film that they went to see.

All the same, she thanked Sadie with genuine fervor for the evening's pleasure, for she felt that, thanks to her, a gleam of hope had appeared on the horizon.

THE NEXT MORNING, however, the idea of appealing to Florian on quite such intimate grounds seemed a little less ingenious that it had the previous evening. Indeed, by the time Marianne reached the boutique, the whole project had taken on such an unpractical air she would have abandoned it entirely, except for one thing.

And that was that, quite unexpectedly, Monsieur Florian arrived nearly an hour earlier than usual.

Madame Rachel was not yet in the boutique. Jeanne

and Célestine were busy arranging stock, and no customer needed attention, when Monsieur Florian passed
through with a brisk but agreeable *"Bonjour."*

Not until he had reached the bottom of the stairs did
Marianne quite come to her senses, and then she acted
on impulse, without allowing herself time to be frightened.

"Monsieur...." She put out her hand, though she
did not actually touch him.

He turned, with one foot on the bottom step, and
looked inquiring—but good-humoredly so.

"Mademoiselle?"

"Monsieur Florian, could I—could I please come and
speak to you privately?"

"I am busy," he began. Then he gave her a penetrating glance. "Is it very important?"

"To me it is, *monsieur*," Marianne said humbly.

He smiled faintly.

"Very well, then. Come upstairs now. But I cannot
give you more than ten minutes."

"It will be enough," Marianne assured him, and she
followed him up the stairs, aware that the other girls
looked after her curiously.

"Well?" Having tossed his hat and coat on to a peg,
and pulled out the chair from behind his desk, he sat
down and waited for Marianne to begin.

"It's about—Lisette, *monsieur*—"

"Not again?" He made a face. "What has Lisette
been doing now?"

"Oh, nothing, Monsieur Florian. It's just that—she is
afraid you are going to dismiss her—"

"Of course," he agreed carelessly. "I wished her to
have an uncomfortable weekend."

"And I do not want Lisette to be dismissed on my
behalf."

"She will not be dismissed on your behalf, *mademoiselle*," Florian assured her dryly. "If she were dismissed
it would be solely because I no longer considered her of
use to my firm."

"Yes, I know," Marianne hastened to assure him.

"But—I know this sounds rather presumptuous, *monsieur*—it would be of—of great help to me if you would tell Lisette that I interceded on her behalf, and that you had decided *not* to dismiss her."

"In consequence of your plea, you mean?" Up went Florian's eyebrows.

"If you would—would be so good, *monsieur*."

"*Mademoiselle,* no one who knew me would believe that I would do such a thing," Florian assured her. "I am not susceptible to pleas and intercessions. To be frank, they bore me."

"Oh, *monsieur*," said Marianne reproachfully, "not if they are well founded, surely?"

"Even then." Florian gave a faint, rather cold smile. "But your proposition intrigues me. Explain yourself."

"Well—" Marianne cleared her throat nervously "—you may not remember, but—"

"There are few things I forget, *mademoiselle*."

"Then you may remember that Lisette and I are—are interested in the same person."

"Of course, of course," Florian agreed impatiently. "This is why she tried to get you into trouble." And he glanced at his watch in a way that reminded Marianne of the fleeting moments.

"Monsieur Florian," she explained in a hasty outburst of eloquence, "Lisette has managed to convince him that it is *I* who have deliberately got *her* into trouble, and that, solely due to my spiteful accusations, she is in danger of losing her job."

"*Mademoiselle,* if he is as gullible as that, there is little we can do about it," Florian said, beginning to open his mail.

"But," persisted Marianne desperately, "if you would so very kindly do what I ask, my role will be completely changed. I would no longer be Lisette's accuser but her—in a way, her rescuer."

"And you think that would impress him?" Florian sounded skeptical.

Suddenly unable to speak, Marianne just nodded. And after a moment he looked up and saw her distress.

"*Petite,* he is not worth it," the Frenchman said, with not unkind cynicism.

"To me he is, *monsieur,*" Marianne replied, almost in a whisper. "And—you don't know him."

"True. But I deplore his judgment," returned Florian with a shrug. "However, it is not necessary that I should admire him. This I recognize. And, since you are a good child—" he smiled at her suddenly "—I will do what you ask."

"Oh, *monsieur!*"

"But if you seriously suppose that Lisette will be grateful, or will help you to turn this to your own account, you are almost too naive to qualify for work in my boutique."

"Oh, *monsieur!*" said Marianne again, but in a different tone.

"That being so," went on Florian, "I must at least see that you benefit by all this effort." And drawing a sheet of paper toward him, he began to write in a bold, rapid hand.

Marianne watched him puzzledly, and when he finally handed her the sheet of paper, she read it curiously. Then, as the full meaning of what he had written dawned upon her, she gave an incredulous little laugh of surprise and joy.

The message was written on a memorandum sheet and simply said:

Mademoiselle Marianne, it is not customary for my staff to write letters to me on personal matters. But, since you make such a point of it—and since, after all, you were the person injured—I will respect your plea on Madamoiselle Lisette's behalf and withdraw the notice of dismissal that I was about to give to her.

Florian.

"Monsieur Florian, how good of you! How—how wonderful. You are the best and kindest of employers!" exclaimed Marianne.

"On the contrary, I am aware that I have sometimes been described as a monster," replied Florian dryly. "However, I am glad if this pleases you. Now, *mon enfant,* please go back to your work. I have a very busy morning in front of me."

So with renewed thanks, and an indescribably lightened heart, Marianne returned to the boutique, carrying with her the precious slip of paper that would show even the obstinate Nat that she had acted generously toward Lisette.

Apparently Florian must have convinced even Lisette of the fact, because toward the end of the afternoon she came to Marianne and, a little sulkily, said, "Monsieur Florian says I am to thank you for interceding on my behalf."

"Oh, Lisette—" Marianne was half amused, half put out "—that's all right. Let's forget about it, shall we?"

"There are some things that one does not forget," replied Lisette enigmatically. Then she went away upstairs again, leaving Marianne undecided as to whether she was referring to injuries or benefits.

But all uncomfortable reflections were dispelled when, half an hour later, Marianne was summoned to the telephone and it was Nat's voice that greeted her.

"Oh, Nat—I'm so glad you called!" she exclaimed.

"I felt I must. We parted on a pretty unsatisfactory note on Saturday, didn't we?"

"Yes, I felt that, too," Marianne agreed gravely. For, with Florian's justification in her handbag, she had no reason to start apologizing at this point.

"I thought—Marianne, can I see you this evening?"

She supposed it would not be a bad thing if she appeared to hesitate about that. But it was not in her to do so.

"Yes, of course," she said, still in that grave tone. A tone that she hoped befitted one who made generous and handsome gestures.

"Eight o'clock outside the front of the Opéra? I don't think I can manage anything earlier."

"I'll be there," Marianne promised. "Will you pick me up in the car?"

"No. It's out of commission for a day or two. I'll be waiting on the steps."

"Very well," she said. And then, knowing they were busy in the boutique with Marcelle still away, Marianne said goodbye hastily and went back.

During the last hour of the day she was too busy to think much about her own affairs. But when she was at last released, she left the boutique with an eager step, her eyes bright and a little smile of happy anticipation lifting the corners of her mouth.

This time it was going to be all right! No more ill-judged criticisms or expressions of opinion. One was not often given such a chance to retrieve a lost situation, and this evening, Marianne told herself, Nat and she would rise above all past misunderstandings.

She could hardly wait for the happy moment when she would greet him on the steps of the Opéra. And she could hardly wait for the moment when she would casually show him the words that Florian had so thoughtfully written.

Really, Florian was a darling! No one was going to be allowed to call him a monster in her presence ever again. Without his help—

But there was no need to think about that. She had *had* his help. And that was why she was hurrying home now with a sense of joyous confidence, to change into her very prettiest dress for her meeting with Nat.

She had started by thinking she had a good deal of time to spare. But when she reached her lodging, she found a long letter from her mother. And by the time she had read this and done one or two necessary chores, suddenly it was perilously near the hour for her rendez-vous with Nat.

She changed hurriedly and was just adding the finishing touches when Sadie knocked on her door and said, "There's someone downstairs, asking to see you—waiting in the parlor."

It must be Nat, come to fetch her, after all.

"I'm coming—I'm coming!" Marianne called back, with a little lilt of happiness in her voice. And, catching up her gloves and bag, she came out of her room, flashed a radiant smile at Sadie and then ran downstairs to the rather depressing sitting room that was known throughout the house as "the parlor."

It wasn't really a place for lovers to meet, for there was not a grain of glamour about its faintly musty austerity. But Marianne flung open the door with a smile—and then stopped dead.

For it was not Nat who was waiting for her. It was Marcelle who got slowly to her feet and stood there, looking curiously without direction or purpose.

"Marcelle," Marianne said, nonplussed and disturbed. "Marcelle—what is it, dear? Is something wrong?"

"Yes," the other girl said, in an exhausted little voice. "It's *maman*. She's dead."

CHAPTER TEN

"OH, MY DEAR—" Marianne came forward and took Marcelle's slack hands in hers "—I'm so terribly sorry. Sit down." She gently put the other girl into one of the few comfortable chairs in the room and knelt down beside her. "Now tell me. It must have been very sudden."

"Yes." Marcelle nodded. She held tightly to Marianne's hand and appeared to derive some sort of comfort and support from the contact. "Early this morning *maman* seemed suddenly much worse. She didn't speak at all." And Marcelle gave a little shake of her head, as though she found it impossible to describe how strange the shabby little apartment became without the sound of *maman's* querulous voice asking for things.

"I knew she was not asleep, and yet I couldn't get her to say anything. I called the doctor, and when he came he said she must go to hospital at once. I went with her, of course, and I stayed all day. She died half an hour ago."

"Marcelle dear—" Marianne put her arm around the pathetic figure "—at least she was in no pain?"

"Oh, no. It was just so—so strange that she was so quiet." Marcelle leaned her head back against the chair and looked exhausted. "And—I felt I couldn't go back to the apartment alone. I thought the only thing was to come to you. You've always been so kind to me," she explained simply.

"Oh, Marcelle—" Marianne was touched to find that her almost casual good humor and kindness could appear in such a light "—I never did very much for you. But of course you were quite right to come to me. I'm afraid it's not very comfortable or private here—'' She glanced around. "Would you like to come up to my room? At least you can lie down on the bed there."

"Yes, please." Marcelle looked grateful. "I don't know why—for I have done nothing all day—but I feel so tired."

"Of course you do. It's the emotional strain," Marianne told her. And, taking Marcelle's arm, she escorted her upstairs to the pleasant attic room that she had contrived to make very comfortable and home-like.

"You lie on the bed and—"

"I can't sleep," Marcelle said quickly. "Stay and talk to me, Marianne. I've been alone so long. At least, not exactly alone at the hospital. But they were all strangers."

"I know. I'll stay," Marianne promised soothingly. But she could not forbear a distracted glance at her watch, for suddenly—and with the utmost dismay—she had remembered Nat, who must have been waiting for some time now, on the steps of the Opéra.

"Is it all right?" Abnormally sensitive to any sign of not being welcome, Marcelle looked worried immediately. "Perhaps you were going out somewhere? In fact, of course you were!" For the first time she appeared to take in the fact that Marianne was wearing her hat and coat. "I'd better go." And she started to get off the bed.

"Certainly not." Marianne gently put her back. "You stay where you are. I was going out, but it's really of no importance." (If only she could have telephoned Nat somewhere!)

"Were you going to meet someone?" Marcelle asked quickly.

"Yes, but—"

"Where?"

"Outside the Opéra. But it's all right. He'll guess something has kept me. He might even—"

"Oh, I'm so sorry!" Marcelle, who had spent a good

deal of her life apologizing to *maman,* now began to apologize abjectly for her very presence.

"It doesn't *matter,*" Marianne insisted. "And anyway, I know what I'll do. I'll get my next-door neighbor, Sadie, to go and explain. You lie still and I'll arrange it with her."

And, a good deal reassured by the idea, she went out and knocked on Sadie's door.

"Come in," called Sadie's cheerful voice. And when Marianne entered, she looked up and said, "Hello! I thought you were going out with one of your beaus."

"I was. But something has happened." Rapidly Marianne explained. "And I wondered whether—Sadie, will you be an angel and go over to the Opéra and try to find Nat and explain? Have a taxi, on me—but please go quickly. It—it's important that he shouldn't think I'm giving him the brushoff."

"Yes, of course." Sadie was already putting on her coat. "How do I know him from all the other people waiting on the steps of the Opéra?"

"Oh, there can't be so many, surely! He's tall and dark and very lively looking. And he'll probably be looking at his watch every five seconds in an impatient sort of way."

"I see. Has he been waiting a very long time, then?"

"It won't be too impossibly long if you manage to get a taxi. But I'd already cut it a bit fine, and I must have been talking to Marcelle for some time. Let me give you the fare—"

"No, no. Settle later. And anyway, I haven't got the taxi yet," Sadie pointed out with a touch of pessimism.

"That's true." Marianne bit her lip, for that taxi could make all the difference—and this was not the best time in the evening to pick one up. However, it was a relief to see Sadie start down the stairs at a quick, light run. And then Marianne returned to her own room, where she found Marcelle sitting up, her head in her hands.

"Darling. . . ." Marianne sat down on the side of the

bed. But when the other girl dropped her hands, Marianne saw that she was not crying.

"It's all right." Marcelle smiled faintly at her. "I'm just trying to—to get used to things. And—I know it seems dreadfully insensitive to say so, but I'm so *hungry*, Marianne."

"Good heavens! I'm so sorry, I didn't think. Didn't they give you anything at the hospital?"

"I believe they offered me something once, but I couldn't think about it then. Now...." She broke off.

"Don't worry. I can rustle up something quite easily," Marianne promised.

And in less than ten minutes she had some hot soup ready and had cooked Marcelle an excellent omelet over her useful little gas ring.

"Oh, it's lovely!" Marcelle drew a long sigh of relief and satisfaction, and a little color began to creep back into her cheeks as she buttered crusty bread and did full justice to Marianne's omelet. "You're so kind, Marianne. Almost like a—a sister."

Marianne bent forward and kissed her lightly. And she tried not to think too much about Nat, or the kind of explanation he might well be finding for her nonappearance.

I should have sounded more cordial on the phone, she thought remorsefully. *How silly to stand on my dignity like that! As though it mattered. I shouldn't have left so much to be explained when we met. He wasn't at all convinced that everything was all right again between us. And now, when I just don't turn up, he'll think— Oh, what will he think?*

Marcelle had begun to talk again now, like someone who had kept her thoughts so long to herself that, given the opportunity, she now *had* to talk, even if she repeated herself—which she did, rather often.

Patiently, Marianne listened all over again to the story of *maman*'s usual reactions and the strangeness of life when these suddenly changed. But she saw that Marcelle was growing sleepy now, in a quieter, more contented sort of way that was very different from the tense exhaustion she had first shown.

I have to keep her for the night, Marianne thought suddenly. *It's quite impossible for the poor little thing to go back to her own apartment alone. And where else can she go?*

"Listen, dear—" Marianne cut across the story that was growing rather rambling now "—I'm going to get you to bed. You'll sleep here for tonight, and we'll think about something else in the morning."

"Here, in this bed?" Marcelle was divided between relief and a vague idea that she should apologize again for giving so much trouble. "But where will you sleep?"

"I can make up a sort of chair bed," Marianne declared. "No arguments! I can lend you everything you need. I even have a spare toothbrush!" And she smiled indulgently at Marcelle, as though she were a child. "Tonight I make the decisions."

"Oh, how wonderful!" The relief of not having to make any decisions almost reduced Marcelle to tears. But, with a sort of brisk cheerfulness Marianne contrived to keep her attention on the simple matter of getting ready for bed. And very soon she had the satisfaction of seeing Marcelle, already half-asleep, tucked up comfortably for the night.

After that there was nothing to do but sit and wait until Sadie should return. With reassuring news—or without it.

It seemed a long time, though it could not really have been so, Marianne knew, before Sadie's footsteps were heard coming rapidly upstairs. Marianne went out onto the landing, the door behind her. And, as soon as Sadie's bright head appeared above the level of the stairs, she asked anxiously, "Well?"

"I'm sorry." Sadie shook her head, and she was panting a little from the rapidity of her ascent. "I gave him ten minutes, in case he could have gone away to phone and then come back. But there was no one there, Marianne."

"No one?"

"Well, I mean no one who could possibly have been your Nat. There was an old fellow of at least fifty—" for thus did Sadie view the middle-aged "—and a couple of girls, and a peasanty sort of guy who couldn't have been anything but French. No one in the least like your man. But I hardly expected it," she added. "For I couldn't get a taxi all the way, Marianne. By the time I got there I felt pretty sure he must have given it up."

"Yes—I see." Marianne tried to look philosophical. "Well, it can't be helped."

"Perhaps he'll phone," Sadie suggested.

"Perhaps." But she knew he wouldn't phone. She knew Nat thought she didn't want to see him anymore. And it was even possible that he would console himself by spending the evening with Lisette.

She thanked Sadie for her efforts and went back into her own room. And presently she made up a sort of emergency bed, and there she spent an uncomfortable night, sleeping at intervals but waking every now and then with a crick in her neck, to the sharp awareness that another unfortunate barrier had been erected between herself and Nat.

Marcelle slept exhaustedly and did not wake until Marianne herself was half-dressed. But then she seemed unusually refreshed and lively, and almost embarrassingly grateful for Marianne's friendly care of her.

"It is beyond anything—that you gave up your own bed to me, too," she declared.

"Really, it was nothing." Marianne rubbed a slightly stiff neck absently. "But we'll have to find a better arrangement for the future."

"I can't go back to the apartment alo—"

"No, of course not. You needn't be afraid about that."

"Perhaps," Marcelle suggested wistfully, "I could get a room here, in this house."

"I doubt it." Marianne shook her head. "It's cheap and so it's almost always full. Only yesterday I heard someone being turned away. I could probably get you in here eventually, but it would take some time. However, we'll think of something," she declared, with more confidence than she felt. "And meanwhile, here is breakfast," she added, as the chink of china was heard outside the door.

Some rapid explaining on Marianne's part presently produced coffee and rolls for Marcelle, too, though with a rather bad grace on the part of the landlady, who obviously only half believed the story and strongly suspected that someone had, inconceivably, contrived to have a free night's lodging in her house.

"I hope she didn't mind too much," Marcelle said in a scared whisper.

"I don't care if she did," replied Marianne stoutly. And, after some good hot coffee, Marcelle, too, gathered fresh courage.

So much so that before Marianne could even get so far as asking what she proposed to do that day, she said thoughtfully, "I shall come with you to the boutique, Marianne. It is best that I should work again now. To sit and think is never good. Then later in the day I will ask Madame Rachel to release me, so that I can make arrangements for—for the funeral."

"Have you no family at all, Marcelle?" Marianne looked worriedly at her. "No uncles or cousins or anything?"

"I have a great-aunt in Rouen," said Marcelle despondently. "She is nearly ninety."

"Well, she isn't going to be much help to you at this time. Anyone else?"

Marcelle shook her head.

"Never mind. One can always manage if one has to," Marianne declared, because somehow it is always much easier to be resourceful and philosophical about other people's problems than about your own.

Together the two girls set off for the boutique, through the cool bright sunshine of a perfect early-spring morning, and Marianne was half amused, half touched to see that, in spite of her inevitable gravity, Marcelle from time to time showed a sort of timid flutter of good spirits.

Once she's got over the shock of it all, she's going to be much happier without poor maman, Marianne thought. *And can one wonder? It isn't nice to be entirely alone, of course, but it must have its attractions if one had been subject to a domestic tyrant.*

At the boutique they found a sympathetic audience for their story in Madame Rachel, who in the nicest way possible enjoyed births, marriages and deaths with a good-humored impartiality that belongs to the natural sensationalist. She was truly sorry that one of her staff should be bereaved, but that did not prevent her from welcoming the story on an otherwise dull morning.

Indeed, so well did she play the part of sympathetic fellow mourner that Marcelle began to look much nearer tears than she had at any other time since Marianne had taken her in hand. *"Pauvre petite,"* she called Marcelle, and at the third repetition of this depressing phrase Marcelle really would have burst into tears if at that moment Monsieur Florian had not entered, accompanied—unexpectedly at this early hour—by Madame Florian.

"I came to thank you both for finding my brooch," she began, with her heartwarming smile at Marianne.

But Madame Rachel, in suitably hushed accents, hastened to explain that graver matters had supervened, and in a couple of minutes she had the Florians also involved in the general discussion of Marcelle's affairs.

If Florian was faintly bored—which Marianne secretly suspected—he hid the fact. But it was Gabrielle who immediately became not only sympathetic but practical.

"You lived alone with your mother, didn't you, dear?" she said to Marcelle, who was somewhat restored by the distinction of being thus addressed by Madame Florian. "Have you any other family?"

Madame Rachel, who had even managed to extract the information about the great-aunt by now, answered on Marcelle's behalf, and drew a telling picture of her forlorn and isolated state.

"If the good Marianne had not given up her own bed

last night," she added impressively, "she would have had to sleep alone in the apartment where her dear *maman* died. *La pauvre petite.*"

Marianne wondered if, in the interest of accuracy, she should point out that *maman* had died in hospital, particularly as a faintly ironical gleam had now appeared in Florian's eyes. But Gabrielle said earnestly, "Oh, she can't do that, of course! And nor can Marianne continue to give up her bed. I think—" she bit her lip thoughtfully "—she had better come to us for a few days. Until after the funeral, at any rate. Georges—" she turned to the gravely attentive Florian "—wouldn't that be the best way?"

"If you wish it, *chérie.*" There was a faintly dry note in his voice, but he glanced not unkindly at the flushed and dazzled Marcelle, who suddenly looked anything but "*la pauvre petite.*" "Remember, however, that we have to go out after dinner tonight, and that Marcelle will therefore be alone in *our* apartment then."

"But that's not the same thing at all. Besides—" Gabrielle glanced around, "—perhaps Marianne could spend the evening with her? Then she would not be alone. Could you manage that, *mademoiselle*?"

"Why—why, certainly, *madame,* if you are so kind as to ask me." If Marianne looked slightly less dazzled than Marcelle, she was unashamedly thrilled by the thought of actually being asked visit the Florians in their famous apartment.

"Well, that's settled, then."

"Oh, *madame,* you are indeed an angel!" That was Marcelle, producing her heartfelt, if not very original, description of Gabrielle Florian.

"Not at all." Gabrielle smiled. "We owe you something for finding the brooch, and for all the trouble you had over it. I tell you what I'll do, Marcelle—" suddenly she was very much the eager, unsophisticated English girl who had captured Florian's somewhat cynical heart "—I'll collect you this afternoon, and you and I will go and make all the—the arrangements. It isn't nice to have to do those things alone. Then we will fetch your things and you will come home with me. And Mademoiselle Marianne will come to dinner tonight about seven o'clock. Does that suit everyone?" She glanced around again.

It appeared that this suited everyone so well that there were general smiles. Even Florian produced a dry little smile, and if this concealed a wish that his beloved Gabrielle would sometimes be less warmly impulsive, at least it did conceal the fact very creditably.

Then Florian went upstairs to his office, Gabrielle went about her own affairs, and the boutique returned more or less to normal, except that no one knew quite whether to commiserate with Marcelle on the loss of *maman* or congratulate her enviously on the score of her invitation.

At lunchtime Marianne tried to reach Nat by telephone at his office. But she was told that he was away on some assignment and it was not known when he would return.

Perhaps that's just what he told them to say if I called, she thought despondently. And for a moment she almost wished she were not going to the Florian's that evening, so that she could be free to telephone at intervals, in the hope of finding Nat at home.

For Marcelle, however, there were no such qualifications, and when Gabrielle collected her that afternoon from the boutique, it was obvious that she was thrilled and pleased beyond measure.

"Come in good time, Marianne," she whispered eagerly, before she left. "I don't *think* I shall feel shy alone. Certainly not with her. But perhaps with *monsieur*. And you know better how to talk to him."

Do I, thought Marianne. *Perhaps I do get on with him quite well. But—oh, I'd much rather be able to talk well and convincingly to Nat!*

Once more she tried to reach him by telephone, both at his office and at his private number, when she reached home. But she was unsuccessful in both attempts. And so she unhappily pushed him into the back of her mind and tried to concentrate on her unusual evening engagement.

What did one wear if one was going to dine with one of the top designers in Paris? It was quite a problem, Marianne thought, but simplified by the smallness of a fairly well-chosen wardrobe. And in the end she wore a dark blue cocktail dress of impeccable cut but deceptive simplicity, and hoped that Florian would approve.

It was impossible not to feel a slight flutter of nervous excitement on entering the luxurious block of apartments where the Florians lived. And, as the elevator silently glided up to the magnificent top floor, Marianne found her heart beating faster than usual.

A somewhat intimidating manservant admitted her. But then, almost immediately, Gabrielle herself came out into the hall to greet her, and at once Marianne felt at home.

It was, quite simply, the most beautiful place she had ever seen. That it should be elegant and tasteful to the last degree she had expected. She could not imagine that Florian would settle for less. But, as though grafted on to the ultimate in elegant luxury, there was a homelike atmosphere, which, she felt certain, owed its existence to Gabrielle Florian.

"The proportions of the rooms are so wonderful," Gabrielle explained, when Marianne voiced her admiration. "And so is the view—see!" And she swept back fantastically beautiful curtains from one of the great windows, to show Marianne a breathtaking view of Paris by night.

"It's just as beautiful by day," Gabrielle declared, as Marianne caught her breath. "But there's always something magical about endless lights against a dark scene and a night sky. I never tire of it."

"I should think not, indeed! It's all like—like something one might imagine but never hope to see," Marianne said frankly. And, turning to her hostess she added, "It's terribly kind of you to have Marcelle and me here in your lovely home."

"Oh, no!" Gabrielle smiled protestingly. "It's fun to

share one's pleasures. And I know how one can feel alone in Paris. I was in just that position once, though not so tragically placed as Marcelle. But come—we'll join the others. I think your friend is a little bit afraid of my husband when she's on her own. Though, of course," she added, "there isn't any need to be."

Marianne smiled at her curiously.

"Were you never afraid of him, then?" she asked amusedly, before she could stop herself.

But Gabrielle seemed not to resent the question. She gave it her thoughtful consideration and then said, "I suppose—yes, I was occasionally, in the days when I worked for him, and before I fell in love with him. But he's really quite a simple and vulnerable person, you know, under all that business of the inscrutable myth." And she laughed softly, as she led the way into the great salon.

Here they found Marcelle, sitting somewhat far forward on the edge of her elegant chair, in the effort of making light conversation with her host. Both, Marianne thought, were slightly relieved at the entrance of Gabrielle and herself.

But in a faintly formal way Florian was a charming host and, with anyone less solemn than Marcelle, an amusing one, too. It was not, Marianne found, difficult to talk with him and Gabrielle, and she was just beginning to enjoy the situation—and the strange but delicious-tasting drink that Florian had handed her— when the door opened and in came Roger Senloe.

"Roger! How lovely to see you!"

It was Gabrielle who said the words, but they found an immediate echo in Marianne's heart. For to see Roger unexpectedly like this, in slightly alien surroundings, gave her a joyful surprise—almost a shock—like nothing else she had ever experienced.

He looked so handsome, too, standing there in the doorway. So handsome that, if she hadn't known she was in love with Nat and breaking her heart for him, she could almost have rushed forward and embraced him.

However, of course, there was no question of this. In

point of fact, it was Gabrielle's smooth cheek that he
lightly kissed. Then there was a certain amount of explaining, Marcelle was introduced, and presently he was
holding Marianne's hand for a second and greeting her
with a smile.

There was nothing to it, really. And yet it seemed to
Marianne that the evening had taken on an entirely new
meaning.

"I was passing, and really just dropped in for a drink
and a word," Roger explained to Gabrielle and Florian.

But both insisted that he must stay to dinner, and
Marianne held her breath with almost painful anxiety
until she heard him agree to stay. She didn't know quite
why it was so important that he should do so—only that
it was.

The conversation around the dinner table was of a
very general character, but Roger sat beside Marianne,
and somehow she felt that this, too, was important and
made the evening different. And after a while the subject of the missing brooch was mentioned, and he
turned and gave Marianne a very special smile of amusement and understanding.

"Fortunately, that matter has now been disposed of
satisfactorily and finally," commented Florian dryly,
for he was evidently not going to have boutique scandal
discussed around his dinner table.

"Oh, quite," agreed Roger gravely. But he gave
Marianne the slightest suspicion of a wink, and she had
the delicious feeling that they shared an amused and
personal experience.

Later, when the Florians were preparing to go out to
their evening engagement, Roger appeared to be taking
his leave, too. But at the last minute he turned to
Marianne and said, "*My* engagement is only a duty one
at a dull official reception. I'll slip away early, and if
you tell me when to call for you, I'll come and take you
home."

"You really don't need to—" Marianne began. But
he smiled a little obstinately and replied, "Let us say
that I like to. What time shall I come?"

"Don't make it too late," Gabrielle warned. "Marcelle should go to bed early."

Marcelle agreed to this—as, indeed, she would have agreed to any other proposal that Madame Florian might have made on her behalf—and it was finally settled that Roger should return about ten-thirty and escort Marianne home.

When the Florians and he had gone, Marcelle sat down with a long sigh of satisfaction and said, "How kind everyone is. Even Monsieur Senloe, who does not really know me. But then he must be truly noble not to hate Monsieur Florian."

"I don't think Roger's the hating kind," replied Marianne practically.

"But to love Madame Florian and to lose her to someone else! This must be hard." Marcelle shook her head sympathetically.

"Yes, I suppose so," Marianne agreed reluctantly. "But it's five years ago, Marcelle."

"Five years are nothing if you really love someone," Marcelle declared. "And if one once loved Madame Florian, how could one look at anyone else?"

Marianne felt she didn't know the answer to that. And because the fact troubled her oddly, she changed the subject.

The girls had a quiet and pleasant evening together. It was strange, sitting there surrounded by the grandeur of the Florian apartment, but it was undoubtedly very comfortable. And when Marcelle grew tired—which she did fairly early—she took Marianne to see the beautiful guest room that had been put at her disposal.

"I am indeed a fortunate girl," sighed Marcelle, and Marianne felt genuinely glad that she was having this charming interlude to make up for some of the hardest days and nights with *maman.*

Roger arrived promptly at ten-thirty, and after the girls had bidden each other good-night with genuine affection, he took Marianne off in his car. "Your little friend looks quite starry-eyed," he observed. "Not nearly as forlorn and bereaved as one might expect."

"Well, frankly, her mother was a bit of a menace," Marianne explained. "And though she probably doesn't know it yet, there must be an element of relief in her present state of mind. Besides, the Florians are being most awfully kind to her. He really is a jewel of an employer, I must say."

"Not everyone would agree," replied Roger with a grin. "And anyway, I suppose it's easy to be generous if you yourself have everything you want in the world."

"And you think Florian has that?"

"Well, of course! A job he loves, a fortune he can hardly count, and—Gabrielle. What more could a man want?"

"I don't know," said Marianne soberly. And after that she let Roger do most of the talking, for his final question—lightly though it had been spoken—gave her much to think about.

What more could a man want than Gabrielle?

The next day at the boutique was a busy one and—perhaps as a reaction from so much sympathy and commiseration the day before—no one seemed to be in a specially good temper. Marianne herself felt her patience strained rather far once or twice, and for once she actually counted the hours until she could be released.

Not that there was anything special she wanted to do with her evening, she told herself, as she put on her hat and coat. Only it would be something just to be quiet and to try to sort out some of the confusing reactions and impressions that had crowded in on her during the last two days.

She drew a long breath of the keen evening air as she stepped out of the boutique—and then she drew another, quicker breath. For standing just a few yards away, looking momentarily in the other direction, was Nat, and it was impossible to tell in that moment if he was waiting for her or for Lisette.

Then he turned. And from the relief and eagerness that flashed into his face, she knew that he had come for her.

"Marianne!" He came forward and took both her

hands. He even kissed her, right there in the middle of the street—when Lisette might come out at any moment. "You don't know how glad I am to see you. I was worried sick the other evening."

"Oh, Nat, I'm so sorry. It wasn't my fault." She began to explain, rapidly and eagerly, as they walked along arm in arm. And suddenly it was the easiest thing in the world to do so, because it was strangely like old times to have Nat in this mood.

Presently he hailed a taxi, and she never even noticed where they were going, until the taxi stopped outside the Secret de Polichinelle. The sight of the familiar frontage gave her an unpleasant little jar for a moment. But then that passed, like something that belonged to quite a different phase of her life and didn't matter anymore.

She was not quite sure what had happened to her. Only she no longer felt anxious and unhappy where Nat was concerned. She was not ready to agonize over his every mood. She was just there with him and enjoying his company.

The waiter who attended to their order was the very same one who had brought her the meal she could not eat, on that dreadful evening when she had first seen Nat there with Lisette. And at that recollection, and in the strange new mood of ease and relaxation, she heard herself ask, almost amusedly, "And what about Lisette these days? Did she tell—"

"Don't talk to me of Lisette," he said abruptly. "For the last two days I've been asking myself how much of a fool a man can be."

"O-oh—" She looked at him with half amused, half sympathetic curiosity. "She's been—disillusioning, you mean?"

"Do we have to talk about her?"

"Not if you don't want to. What shall we talk about instead?"

"Us, Marianne," he said, and reaching across the table, he took her hand in his. "It's the one subject that matters at the moment, isn't it?"

"I—don't know." She looked down at their clasped

hands, and a strangely disturbing little tremor passed over her. "That depends on what you want to say—about us."

"You know, don't you, darling? And you know that I've wasted so much time over it that the only thing is to say it now, without trimmings—I love you, Marianne, and I want you to marry me."

CHAPTER ELEVEN

THEY WERE the very words she had longed and longed to hear Nat say to her, "I love you, Marianne, and I want you to marry me."

She had left England because of the emptiness of life if she could not have him say them. She had stayed and found work in France because it had suddenly appeared possible that here the miracle might happen. For months and months she had waited, hoped, agonized over those words and all they would mean to her.

Now Nat had said them. And, instead of the tremendous, all-consuming rush of feeling that she should have experienced, she was aware of nothing but a sense of anticlimax, a faintly numb and undecided state of mind in which, incredibly, embarrassment was the principal emotion.

"Marianne...." Nat spoke urgently, almost pleadingly. "You knew that was how I felt, didn't you?"

"No." She seized on the possibility of even a few moments' delay before defining her own attitude. "How should I have known how you felt, Nat? You—you weren't very explicit, were you? I thought—" she groped in her mind for something else that would prolong the discussion and avert a decision "—I thought perhaps you were in love with Lisette."

"Oh, Marianne!" His tone was reproachful. "Don't throw her up at me now, even if I deserve it."

"I wasn't throwing her up at you. I was just telling you how I felt," she explained, quickly and a little defensively.

"About me and Lisette?" A hopeful gleam came into his eyes. "Do you mean that you were a bit jealous? You had no need to be, and I don't deserve that you should be. But if you were, Marianne, it argues that you—cared.''

"I did care," she said slowly. "And—yes, I suppose I was jealous at one time. But not now. I mean," she added confusedly, "it doesn't matter now."

She was shocked when she had said the words, because there was something terribly self-revealing about them. But he took them in a different sense and asked tenderly, "Why doesn't it matter, dear? Because you know now that Lisette is quite unimportant in our scheme of things?''

She looked across at him, and with half her mind and heart she truly wished she could give him the answer he was expecting. But his very choice of words had only served to shed fresh light upon her inexplicable change of feeling, and it was all she could do not to say bluntly, "Not because Lisette is unimportant in the scheme of things, but because *you* are."

That was the shattering discovery that had changed her life and made her feel like someone trying to tread water in a rough sea. She had only to say yes, and Nat was hers.

But she didn't want to say yes.

It was all quite inexplicable, even to herself. But somehow, sometime during the crises of the last few days or weeks, an enormous change had taken place. Her whole scale of values had shifted, and Nat was no longer the center of existence.

She liked him. He would always be someone she remembered with affection as a good friend, from the days when he had been her sister's fiancé and they had gone about together, on those evenings when Yvonne was not available. But beyond that she felt nothing.

It was not that she had any resentment toward him. She had no wish to criticize his recent behavior or reproach him with having treated her shabbily over Lisette. None of that mattered anymore.

It didn't matter! That was what she returned to again and again with ever-increasing astonishment. It didn't matter. And nor, come to that, did Nat matter, she realized, with a sense of guilty amazement.

"Marianne—" he was still watching her anxiously "—Marianne, what is it? You haven't given me any sort of answer. I've asked you to marry me, my dear. Is it so very difficult to find the reply?"

"It was—a few minutes ago," she said, with a sort of desperate candor. "But it isn't now. I'm terribly sorry, Nat—I just don't want to marry you."

"But—why not? What has happened between us? Are you angry with me about something?"

"No, certainly not! I've nothing to be angry about," she declared, with a generosity that came so easily now that he had no power to hurt her. "If I'm angry with anyone it's with myself, for taking so long to understand my own feelings."

"But are you sure you understand them now?" he pressed her. "You—you've changed, haven't you, in a matter of minutes? Why, Marianne?"

"I don't know," she said quite simply. "Only I don't think it was in a matter of minutes, Nat. I think the change had come, quite gradually, over a much longer period. It was only when you put things unexpectedly to the test that—I knew."

"Knew what?" he insisted.

"That you're just not the man for me."

"Who is, then?" he demanded, half-angrily.

"I don't know." She opened her eyes wide. "That's something quite different. One can tell that a man is not one's choice without necessarily being able to specify exactly what type would be."

"Type? Type!" he repeated irritably. "It's not a *type* that has changed your feelings so radically, Marianne. You loved me once—I know you did—in fact, you've as good as said so. Even as recently as the Charities Fair, I was 'the man for you,' to use your own phrase. Wasn't I?"

She hesitated.

"Wasn't I?" he insisted.

"Well, yes," she admitted reluctantly.

"Then what happened?"

"I've told you—I don't know." Suddenly she was frightened, though it was difficult to say why.

"Was it because I was so pigheaded and unreasonable about Lisette?"

"Oh, no." She wished he could understand how utterly unimportant all that had become now. "Lisette doesn't matter, Nat. Really she doesn't."

"And I don't matter, either, do I?" Suddenly the truth of that seemed to strike him, inescapably.

"Of course you do, in a way!" she cried in distress. "You're a good friend and I'm fond of you and I wish you all the good in the world. But I don't want to marry you."

"Even though you did once?"

"Very well. Even though I did once."

"Then there's someone else."

"Of course there's not!" She spoke with more emphasis than was strictly necessary. "How could there be? I hardly *know* anyone else here in Paris. Just the Florians, and the girls at the boutique, and Sadie and—and—"

"And Roger Senloe," he reminded her gloomily.

"Yes—Roger Senloe, of course," she agreed with outward calm, though the mention of his name in this context was suddenly like a blow over the heart.

"Well, then, I suppose it's Senloe."

"Please, Nat, don't be so ridiculous! There's never been a word of—of lovemaking or romance between me and Roger Senloe. He's unshakably devoted to Gabrielle, if you must know."

"Gabrielle? Florian's wife, you mean? Now *you* are being ridiculous! The Florians are famous for their devotion to each other."

"Yes, of course. I didn't mean anything of *that* sort." Her shocked tone appeared to reject any reciprocal feeling of any sort at all on Gabrielle's part. "But Roger was in love with her before she married Florian."

"But that's years ago!"

"I know. But I'm sure he's never changed," Marianne said reverently, as she recalled Marcelle's pronouncements on the impossibility of renouncing a devotion to Madame Florian.

"Well, it sounds a great deal of nonsense to me," Nat declared impatiently. "But it's of only secondary importance. If you're convinced that Senloe's still in love with Gabrielle Florian, you can't be thinking of *him* as 'the man in your life.'"

"Certainly not!" agreed Marianne breathlessly. And immediately a sort of superstitious dread came over her, as though she had said something that invited disaster.

One should never tell a direct lie about the things that mattered most. Only—was this what mattered most? And had she told a lie?

Once more her mind and heart were in a state of indescribable confusion, and it was all she could do to pay attention to Nat when he said almost appealingly, "But if there's no one else, Marianne, it *could* be me again, couldn't it?"

She stared at him, wordless and distressed because she hated hurting him. But then she slowly shook her head.

"I'm frightfully sorry, Nat, dear. And truly I'm not being capricious or difficult. I'm very fond of you as a friend, and once I thought I was in love with you. I *know* now that I'm not. I don't want to keep on laboring the point, because it sounds both rude and unkind— but I don't want to marry you, and I can only tell you that my answer is no. Please can't we leave it at that?"

He couldn't, of course. Or rather, he wouldn't. And during a rather uncomfortable meal he reverted to the topic, in one form or another, several times more. She steered him away from it again as gently as she could, but with ever-increasing conviction that her mind was unshakably made up. She could not and she would not marry Nat.

It was over at last, that unhappy meal together. And at least she managed to convince him that there was no point in their spending any more of the evening together.

He took her home to her lodgings, and he kissed her when they said goodbye. But it was an unhappy, perfunctory kiss, which expressed neither a grand farewell nor a confident promise for the future. She did her best in return. But there is nothing flatter than a duty kiss bestowed where once one loved. And feeling very miserable and inadequate, Marianne murmured a hurried goodbye and fled into the house.

She ran up the stairs, partly because she felt she was escaping from a distasteful situation, and partly from an instinctive longing for action after the passive role she had played.

By the time she reached her top landing she was panting, and Sadie, who had just opened her door to put out an empty milk bottle, looked across at her and laughed.

"Who are you running away from?" she inquired.

"N-no one. Except from myself, perhaps," Marianne added, before she could stop herself.

"Oh?" Sadie's eyebrows went up. "It's like that, is it? Then you'd better come in and have a cup of coffee with me. It's not easy to run away from oneself in one room, without company."

Marianne laughed a little, too, then. But she accepted the offer gratefully. For in some odd way she *had* been running away from herself, and she was still afraid of that final degree of self-knowledge that she knew awaited her as soon as she was alone.

She followed Sadie into her room and gratefully accepted both the comfortable chair and the cup of coffee that were offered.

"So it was a trying evening?" Sadie said, when they had both sipped their coffee in silence for a few minutes.

"It was, rather."

"Do you want to tell me about it?"

"I don't know. Yes, I suppose I'd like to tell someone, and you're nice and discreet."

Sadie looked both startled and impressed that anyone should have this view of her, but Marianne was not noticing her expression. She went on, slowly and thoughtfully, "It was just that—someone proposed to me, and I had to refuse him. That's always distressing, unless you're a quite horrid sort of person."

"I'll say!" agreed Sadie feelingly. "Was it unexpected?"

"I suppose it was—in the end. If it had happened a month ago—" She broke off and was silent, lost in contemplation of that possible state of affairs, and unable to decide whether it would have been a blessing or a major disaster.

Sadie watched her curiously. Then, with what seemed to Marianne a somewhat startling gleam of intuition, she asked, "Was it the guy you sent me to find on the steps of the Opéra?"

"Y-yes, it was, as a matter of fact."

"I thought he was very important to you," said Sadie mildly.

"So did I. In fact, he *was* very important, Sadie. I was crazy about him. Only now—it's over."

"You mean you quarreled?"

"Oh, no. Nothing as dramatic as that. It's just that my feelings have changed. I don't want him anymore."

"Do you want someone else instead?"

"No, certainly not." She was emphatic about that, as she had been to Nat, and for almost a minute there was silence between the two girls.

Then Sadie said kindly, "I suppose the fact is that you've fallen for Florian."

"Fallen for Florian? Good heavens, no! Why ever should I?" Marianne wanted to know.

"Because he's one of the most fascinating men in Paris, according to all accounts. I'm sure I'd be mad about him if I worked for him," declared Sadie comfortably. "I love these enigmatic, authoritative men."

Marianne laughed.

"I didn't know you were so sentimental, Sadie."

"Me? I'm a mass of sentiment," Sadie said, complacently. "But that's neither here nor there. We were really talking about you."

"I don't know that there's anything more to say about me," Marianne observed with a sigh.

"Don't grieve, honey. There'll soon be someone else," Sadie assured her kindly. "You're much too pretty to remain long without a special admirer. Anyway, what about that other fellow—the one who spoke up for you so handsomely when Madame Florian's brooch was lost?"

There was the faintest pause. Then Marianne said, not quite steadily, "Roger Senloe, you mean?"

"Was that the name? He was something in the diplomatic service."

"Yes," said Marianne. And for the life of her there was nothing else she could say.

"What about him?" asked Sadie briskly.

Marianne found herself explaining all over again that all his devotion was expended on Gabrielle Florian, whom he had once hoped to marry. And somehow, as she recapitulated the facts for, admittedly, a more receptive and sentimental audience than Nat, her spirits sank to zero, and below.

"It's a pretty story," observed Sadie pensively, making Marianne immediately glad that Roger could not hear his affairs thus described. "It's unusual for a man to be so faithful to something unattainable."

"Roger *is* unusual," Marianne said, with a touch of pride in her voice. And then suddenly she didn't want to sit there any longer and discuss him with Sadie. She wanted to get away by herself and think—and think—and think.

She thanked Sadie for the coffee and counsel, and declaring that she was tired, she said good-night and went to her own room.

But she was not tired at all. At least, not in the sense of being sleepy. In fact, she had never been more desperately and completely awake. She sat there alone in her own room without even turning on the light, the only illumination provided by an intermittent flashing from an electric sign opposite.

And as the light flashed on and off, it seemed to

Marianne that great flashes of self-knowledge came
with it.

She loved Roger, of course. She had been staving off
the final admission to herself all the evening. That was
why she had eagerly accepted Sadie's invitation. But
now she was face-to-face with the realization.

When Nat said it had to be a personality, not a type,
who had changed her views so entirely, she had known
instinctively that very moment that he was right. It was
Roger who had made all her life mean something different. Nat didn't matter any longer, in the real sense,
because Roger mattered so much.

She had no idea when the final change had taken
place, but with half-melancholy pleasure she retraced
the events of the last few weeks, and it seemed to her
that every scene in which Roger had appeared now took
on a special significance.

Why, it was he who had rescued her from the depths
of despair after her first realization that Nat was interested in Lisette. Even when he was virtually a stranger to
her, he had looked after her and consoled her with a
degree of kindly imagination not to be found in anyone
else she knew. (Rather ungratefully, at this point, she
forgot that Florian also had not done badly so far as
kindly imagination was concerned when he had written
her the note about Lisette. But there was no room for
thoughts of Florian—or indeed anyone but Roger—in
her mind at this moment.)

It was Roger who had stood by her over the unfortunate incident of the brooch, both when it first disappeared and when Florian had questioned her. It was to
Roger she had instinctively—and with justice—turned
when she felt she needed friendly support. And finally,
it was Roger whose appearance in the Florians' apartment, only yesterday, had made her feel suddenly light-
hearted and happy and strangely excited.

How typical of him to make that kindly offer to
return to the apartment and take her home. How easily
and intimately they had talked on the way, until—

Suddenly, and with deepest dismay, she recalled what

he had said when they spoke of Florian's good fortune in his work, his success and his marriage.

What more could any man want, Roger had said musingly, if he had Gabrielle?

It had shaken her at the time, though she hardly knew why. Now the rhetorical question seemed full of the direst significance. For alas, if it meant anything, it meant that Marcelle was all too right. If one truly loved, then one didn't get over it in five years—and if one loved Gabrielle Florian, how could one ever look at anyone else? That was Marcelle's opinion. And, in essence, that was what Roger's words meant.

For a long time Marianne sat there, trying to read some other meaning into the remark, but without success. To Roger she was just a nice, hardworking girl in the boutique at Florian's. Pleasant to know, worthy of support when she got into a scrape, and perhaps to be regretted occasionally if she slipped out of his life without further incident. But more than that—

And she *wanted* more than that! Much, much more than that. She wanted him to love her, in the half humorous, half romantic way he loved Gabrielle. Even more than that. She wanted him to love her so ardently, so intensely, that he forgot he had ever been in love with Florian's wife.

Daydreams—and it's nearly midnight, she told herself half-scornfully. And she tried to pretend that she was almost amused at her own absurdity. But she was really so little amused that she had to wipe away a few tears before she got up, with a sigh, put on the light at last and began to prepare for bed.

THE NEXT DAY at the boutique was inexplicably busy, almost as busy as the first few days after the showing of the new collection. It sometimes happened that way. An especially fine day would bring extra people into town, or an influx of foreign visitors would converge on the fascinating square mile that contains most of the great fashion houses. There was no accounting for these

things. But such a day always meant a great deal of
work, a great deal of interest, probably a drastically cur-
tailed lunch hour, and finally, a considerable amount of
clearing up after the last customer had gone.

By now Marianne was not only entirely a familiar
figure with every detail of the stock, but also a real support for Madame Rachel. All the assistants were good, in
their varied ways. But Florian had been right, as usual,
when he picked Marianne. In a relatively short time she
had become a key worker in the boutique, and it was to
her that Madame Rachel tended to turn in an emergency.

"Marianne, this evening I have to leave early," she
explained, "and to you I will entrust the final checking
and clearing up. The little Marcelle can help you, if you
wish, but to you I delegate the final responsibility."

Wondering, not for the first time, why it was that
both Madame Rachel and Madame Moisant could in-
vest even routine matters with the importance of a state
funeral, Marianne promised to see that all was attended
to correctly. And when the others had gone, she sent off
Marcelle, too.

"I can manage perfectly well," she declared, "and
you still need to catch up on some of the lost rest of the
past few weeks."

"I do not mind being tired if it will help you,"
declared Marcelle, who had inherited a slight taste for
martyrdom from *maman*.

Marianne, however, said emphatically and a trifle
dryly that having Marcelle tired would be of no help to
her whatever, and remembering that she might thus
have a quiet half hour with Gabrielle before Monsieur
Florian came home, Marcelle then took herself off.

Alone in the boutique, Marianne worked rapidly and
efficiently, soothed by the comparative silence around
her. After the feverish activity of the day it was pleasant
to be the only one in the place, and although there were
still sounds of coming and going in the salon overhead,
distance muted these so that they were not disturbing.

Occasionally someone would come running down the

stairs and pass through the boutique with a casual good-
night. And once, when it was Lisette, there was no
good-night at all. She went through as though Marianne
was part of the boutique fittings.

But once again Marianne reflected that Lisette had
lost all power to hurt, or even to annoy her. And she
went on with her work until Florian himself came downstairs and paused to say, "You're working late, *mademoiselle*."

"I've nearly finished, *monsieur*. It's been a very busy
day."

"Upstairs, too," agreed Florian, with an air of satisfaction. "All goes very well this season."

"So it seems, *monsieur*." And Marianne smiled at
him, because she liked him and was pleased that he
should look gay and satisfied, instead of tired and faintly worn, as he sometimes could.

It seemed that her friendly feeling must have con-
veyed itself to him. For instead of saying good-night
and passing on, he lingered for a moment and asked
good-humoredly, "And your own affairs,
mademoiselle? Do they also go well?"

"My—affairs, *monsieur*?"

"The romance," he amplified. "With Monsieur
Nat—of the poor judgment and most unattractive
name. Was he impressed by the note I wrote for his
benefit?"

"Oh, well—" she felt confused when she thought
how drastically things had changed since that note had
been written "—I didn't have to use it, after all, Monsieur Florian."

"You didn't?" He seemed faintly disappointed at not
having been the *deus ex machina,* after all. "How was
that?"

She made an effort to remember.

"He apologized before I could even produce the
note."

"Come, that was most satisfactory, was it not?"

She hesitated. Then she said, but without conviction,
"Yes—certainly, *monsieur*."

He narrowed his eyes slightly and regarded her curiously.

"But the happy ending has still not been achieved?" he suggested.

Marianne looked down at the gloves she was arranging in the case in front of her, and nervously smoothed the top pair.

"N-no, *monsieur*," she said, almost in a whisper. "At least. . . ." She stopped.

"At least—what?" he inquired, with that good-humored curiosity that he sometimes displayed toward his staff, when he had time to think about them as individuals at all. "I think you have no reason to look so dejected, *petite*. Depend upon it, Monsieur Nat is really yours. Lisette's air of triumph is distinctly dimmed these days."

"Yes—I know." She wondered again how she had ever rated Lisette's importance so high that she had actually communicated that valuation to someone else.

There was a second's pause. Most employers would have gone home at that point. But Florian was not like most employers. It was not in him to leave something uncompleted.

"You're not really confident about Monsieur Nat?" he said kindly. "You do not think he will propose in the next few weeks?"

"Monsieur Florian," she was impelled into replying, "he—he *has* proposed." And she looked intensely miserable.

"*Eh bien.*" He looked intrigued. "Is this not a matter for satisfaction—for elation, even?"

She shook her head slowly.

"Why not?"

"I—I don't want him, *monsieur*," she said, again almost in a whisper, and an unexpected tear trickled down her cheek and dropped onto the expensive gloves.

To Florian's credit, he merely leaned over and removed the case from the danger zone without uttering a reproof. Instead, he asked kindly, "Then what—or perhaps I should say whom—do you want, *mon enfant*?"

She couldn't tell him, of course. She just stood there, fighting to keep back her tears. And, after a moment, he said on a somewhat odd note, "Roger!"

Marianne nodded and swallowed a lump in her throat.

"How did you know, *monsieur*?" she said huskily.

"How did I know what, *petite*?"

"That it was R-Roger, and not Nat."

"I didn't know," he said gently. "I was merely greeting Roger, who has just come in."

"*Oh!*" She swung around in horror to see Roger standing just inside the doorway, regarding the scene with such a quizzical air that it was impossible to tell how much he had heard—or understood.

CHAPTER TWELVE

"WHAT'S GOING *on* here?" Roger moved forward, a slight frown on his handsome face. "Have you been bullying Marianne again, Florian?"

"I never bully my employees," replied Florian coldly.

"Of course you do! In your own special way," retorted Roger. "You even bullied the life out of Gabrielle once. What is it, child?" He came close to Marianne and looked down at her with concern. "Has Florian—"

"On the word of Mademoiselle Marianne herself, I am the best and kindest of employers," observed Florian, a trifle complacently, "and if you heard anything of our conversation at all, you must have realized that I was certainly not the one causing her distress."

"I heard nothing of the conversation." Roger spoke deliberately, and Marianne drew a quick gasp of relief. "But I'm not prepared to see Marianne in tears and not know the reason why."

"Oh, R-Roger, it was nothing to do with Monsieur Florian—really." Marianne had recovered her voice at last. "I'm sorry to be so stupid, but—Monsieur Florian was k-kindly asking after my personal affairs and I—I was telling him about something that caused me a—" she swallowed "—a bit of distress."

"I see." Roger glanced from one to the other. "Is there anything I can do to help?"

"No, nothing, thank you," Marianne said quickly. But Florian spoke at almost the same moment.

"Indeed, yes," he said, with that sudden and extraordinarily attractive smile of his. "If you have the evening free, my dear Roger, you are the very person who can help. Marianne is feeling dejected; she had already worked too long. What she needs now is a good meal and some sympathetic company. In my view—"

"All right, Florian." Roger spoke good-humoredly, but with firmness. "I can make my own arrangements. Don't let's keep you. I'm sure Gabrielle's waiting dinner for you now."

"You are right," agreed Florian, with a perfunctory glance at his watch. "Good night, my dear fellow. Good night, Marianne."

"Good night, *monsieur*," said Marianne and watched him go. Then she turned to Roger and said quickly, "I'm terribly sorry. He shouldn't have wished me onto you like that. There's no need to take—"

"He didn't wish you onto me," Roger interrupted quietly. "I was passing the boutique, and when I saw you were still here, I came in to ask you myself if you would come out to dinner with me. Someone had left the outer door ajar—"

"That would be Lisette," she murmured in parenthesis. "She's very careless." And then, wistfully, "Did you *really* come in here with the intention of taking me to dinner?"

"I did, Marianne. Is that so extraordinary?"

"No. Just—nice." She flashed a quick smile at him.

"Good. How much longer will you be?"

"Only a few minutes." Suddenly she was galvanized into quick, even joyous activity. "Sit down, Roger. I really won't be long."

So he took a seat and watched her with a certain degree of satisfaction, as she whisked around, clearing away the last items. Then she ran upstairs with the keys, so that the last person in authority from the salon could lock up. And in very little longer than she had said, she was ready to go out with him.

"Are we going anywhere special?" she inquired, as he helped her into the car.

And she noticed that he smiled slightly as he said, "Quite special. You'll know it when we get there."

But when he finally stopped the car, she could not see any familiar restaurant. Indeed, as she got out of the car, she saw they were on a deserted stretch of the river-bank.

"Why, Roger—"

"Remember?" he said. And, as they walked together toward an empty seat, recollection flooded back upon her.

"Why—it's the very seat where we first met!" she exclaimed.

"Where we first spoke to each other, at any rate," he amended with a smile "I first saw you in the boutique. And then later in the same evening—here. You were crying, because you thought the only man who mattered was interested in someone else."

"S-so I was." She laughed doubtfully, and looked faintly puzzled, like someone who recalled—though imperfectly—some long-past experience.

She sat down on the bench, and he stood looking down at her, his hands in his pockets, his glance very intent upon her. And suddenly he said, in an almost conversational tone of voice. "Marianne, what did you mean back there in the boutique, when you said to Florian, 'It's Roger—it's not Nat'?"

"Oh!" Her hand flew to her lips, in consternation. "Roger, you insisted you didn't overhear anything we said."

"Because I saw your dismay at the idea that I might have done so. I wasn't going to humiliate you in front of Florian."

"Do you want to—humiliate me now?" she asked in a low voice.

"No, darling, of course not." He sat down beside her and put his arm around her. And when she trembled slightly he inquired anxiously, "Are you cold?"

"No, I'm not cold. Only a little—scared of the questions you seem likely to ask."

"I'm sorry. I won't ask questions. I'll tell you something instead, shall I?"

"What are you going to tell me?"

"That I love you, and that I think you're the most

adorable girl in Paris—or the rest of the world, come to that.''

"Roger!" She turned sharply and looked into his face. "You're simply saying that to save my pride!"

"Darling," he replied soothingly, "do you really think any man proposes for such a silly reason as that?"

"N-no. I suppose not." She dropped her head against his shoulder for a moment, and tried to tell herself that this was just a wonderful, wonderful dream and that she must be prepared to wake up and face the disappointment in a minute.

And yet there was something very real and undreamlike about the roughness of his coat against her cheek.

"I thought," she said in a whisper, "that you loved Gabrielle."

"So I did once."

"Does one ever really get over anything like that?" she asked unhappily. "How does one *know* it's over?"

He didn't break into protestations. He merely said thoughtfully, "Do you remember the last time we sat on this seat together?"

"Yes."

"Do you remember exactly what you felt like?"

"I think so."

"About Nat?"

"Oh. . . ." She stopped. Then she went on bravely, "I was mad about him. I thought if he really loved Lisette I didn't know how I could go on. Nothing else in the world seemed to matter. And then you came—and were very kind."

"There was a time when I loved Gabrielle," he told her reflectively. "I was mad about her. I thought if she married Florian I didn't know how I could go on. Nothing else in the world seemed to matter. I've had much longer to get used to the idea, of course, than you have. But, even up to a few months ago, it was extraordinary how the wound could ache sometimes. And then you came."

"Oh, Roger—was it really like that?" She reached

her arm across him and gently stroked the other sleeve of his coat.

"Just exactly like that," he assured her. "But go on. What happened to you after that?"

"You—you know." She laughed slightly. "I went on thinking I was crazy about Nat. I suppose I *was* crazy about him. Right up to last evening, when he asked me to marry him—"

"Good Lord! Did the fellow really come to the point at last?"

"Roger!"

"Sorry. Go on."

"There isn't much more. Except that—I didn't want him. I can't tell you how or why it happened. I just didn't want him. And then—in the boutique tonight—" she faltered a little "—Florian asked me about—my affairs."

"Damned inquisitive of him," observed Roger dryly.

"Oh, no! He meant it very nicely. And—and I told him."

"You said the sweetest words any man ever overheard." He kissed the tip of her ear lightly. "You said, 'It's Roger—it's not Nat.'"

"And was *that* the moment when you—you decided to...." She hesitated again, divided between hope so delicious that she dared not entertain it, and a skepticism so deeply rooted that she could not ignore it.

"No," he said deliberately. "It was a few minutes earlier that the full revelation came to me. You didn't know it, but I stood and watched you for some minutes through the boutique window. And as you moved about so lightly and gracefully, your dear little face so grave and thoughtful, I felt the most extraordinary sensation come over me.

"I remembered—but in a dreamlike sort of way— that there'd been a time when I watched for Gabrielle through that very same window. I tried, quite deliberately, to recapture the feeling—and I couldn't. It was gone, like yesterday's shower. I could only think, 'It's Marianne—it's not Gabrielle.'"

"Oh, Roger!" She flung her arms around him, and he gave her a long kiss on her lips.

They were silent for quite a few moments. Then he said, as though he had to recall the whole scene, "Then Florian came down and began to talk to you. And I saw you look distressed—and I could have killed him."

"Oh, Roger, there was no need. He was being very kind. Do you think he knew you were watching?"

"I expect so. Florian knows most things," Roger said with a humorous shrug of resignation. "In fact—yes, of course. He glanced up, and I suppose he noticed that the door was ajar. Anyway, he made a slight sign for me to come in."

"He did? Florian summoned you in at just that moment!" She gave an incredulous little laugh. "Then he *knew*. I mean—he knew it was you and not Nat, even before I said the words. And he arranged for you to overhear me say as much. He really does take a bit too much on himself!"

"I don't expect it was as cut-and-dried as that," Roger said comfortably. "Though Florian does rather fancy himself as the one who pulls the strings. But anyway, it doesn't matter, does it, darling? Nothing matters now, except that we've found each other."

And to judge from the radiant affection and admiration in her eyes, one might have supposed this was the first time the well-worn phrases had been used between a man and a woman. They sat there talking for some while longer, their arms around each other, their whole beings warmed by an inner glow of happiness that made them quite impervious to the chill night air. But at last, as she held up her face for yet another kiss, a splash of rain fell on her cheek, and Roger exclaimed, "Good heavens, what are we doing, sitting here in the rain without any thought of dinner? Florian said that was what you were most in need of."

"Even Florian doesn't know absolutely everything," she declared with a laugh. But she willingly gave him her hand, and ran with him to the shelter of the car.

They dined in the cozy, intimate little place with the

checked cloths and the superb food. And it never oc-
cured to him that once he had brought Gabrielle here,
nor to her that it was here that she had first told him
about her love for Nat.

For a long time the world seemed to be made up of
themselves and their own entrancing affairs.

But when they had finished their meal and lingered
long enough over their coffee, he said indulgently,
"What would you like to do now? I suppose it's too late
for any kind of show."

"I don't want any kind of show," she assured him.
"Nothing made-up could be half as romantic and wonderful as the truth tonight. But..." she paused, and a
reflective look came into her eyes. "Do you know what
I would really like?"

"No."

"If it's not too late, I would like us to call in and see
the Florians—and tell them our news."

"Would you?" The smile deepened and was touched
by a hint of amused understanding. For perhaps he
knew, even better than she, that what she wanted was
the final reassurance of being there when he told Gabrielle that he was in love with another girl.

"Come along, then." He got up, still smiling. "We'll
go and tell them."

"You don't think it's too late?" she said anxiously,
as though she would have hung back at the last moment.

"No, it's not too late," he assured her.

So together they went to the luxurious block where
the Florians had their home, and were borne aloft in the
silent elevator, and admitted to the apartment by the
intimidating manservant. Only he didn't seem quite
so intimidating now that she had Roger with her.

"It's all right. We'll announce ourselves," Roger
said. And together they entered the beautiful long drawing room.

They stood for a moment in the doorway, taking in
the picture of Gabrielle and Marcelle talking quietly on
either side of the fire while Florian wrote at a desk by
the window.

Then suddenly Gabrielle saw them and sprang to her feet.

"Darling Roger! Darling Marianne!" She rushed toward them and embraced them impartially. "You came yourselves to tell us! How wonderful of you."

"Came to tell you what?" inquired Roger, smiling down at her with the cheerful affection of a taken-for-granted relative. "What's the news?"

"Oh!" She stood back for a moment, looking appalled. "Don't tell me I've made an awful gaffe."

Roger laughed.

"Fortunately—no. Marianne and I are engaged."

"Oh, I'm so happy for you both!" exclaimed Gabrielle, from the bottom of a loving and generous heart, and she kissed Marianne once more.

"But—how did you know?" Laughing and indescribably, immeasurably relieved, Marianne kissed her back again.

"Georges told me."

"Monsieur Florian? But he didn't *know*. It hadn't happened when we last saw him."

She looked across the room at Florian, who had turned from his desk and was regarding the scene with an air of benevolent amusement.

"It did not require a magician to read the signs, *mon enfant*," he said with a shrug. "When Roger hustled me off home it was obvious what he wanted to say, and I could not help thinking that I knew your answer. I congratulate you both with all my heart."

It was Marcelle's turn then to kiss Marianne, and Florian declared that they must all drink to the health of the engaged couple.

"Satisfied?" whispered Roger mischievously, as Florian went to the other end of the long room to pour the drinks.

"To the last, last degree," she whispered back again, giving him an ecstatic and strangely grateful little hug.

Then, as he turned to answer some eager query of Gabrielle's, she slipped from his clasp and followed Florian to the other end of the room.

"Monsieur Florian, I think I owe you an apology."
She stood before him, smiling but a trifle diffident.

"An apology?" He paused in the act of pouring the
drinks and looked inquiring.

"You told me, when you first hired me, that you
didn't want anyone who would marry soon and leave
you."

"True." He smiled faintly. "You have perhaps been
a little thoughtless about my interests in this matter. But
there are exceptions to every rule. This, I think, must be
regarded as an exception."

"Oh, Monsieur Florian, thank you. You—you've
been terribly kind altogether about this. You even
helped things along, didn't you?"

"I, *ma chère*?" He gave her an admirably surprised
glance.

"You called Roger into the boutique at exactly the
right moment, *monsieur*—didn't you?"

"The timing was good," he admitted, without false
modesty.

"Oh, *monsieur*—" she laughed, half reproachfully,
half admiringly "—why did you take it on yourself to
help Roger and me to—to find each other?"

He had filled the glasses now, and setting down the
decanter, he turned to face her.

"I will tell you, *petite*," said Florian, "and it is between you and me only. It has always been a little on my
conscience that it was I who married the loveliest girl
who ever passed through my salon. Now my conscience
is clear, for my good friend Roger Senloe is going to
marry the most charming girl who ever adorned my
boutique."

One book by a favorite author
is a treasure!

Three books
by a
favorite author
is a

**Harlequin
Omnibus**

Three great love stories
in one giant-sized volume —
A book to cherish!

TAKE THESE 4 Harlequin Romances FREE

Thrill to romantic, aristocratic Istanbul, and the tender love story of a girl who built a barrier around her emotions in ANNE HAMPSON's "Beyond the Sweet Waters" . . . a Caribbean island is the scene setting for love and conflict in ANNE MATHER's "The Arrogant Duke" . . . exciting, sun-drenched California is the locale for romance and deception in VIOLET WINSPEAR's "Cap Flamingo" . . . and an island near the coast of East Africa spells drama and romance for the heroine in NERINA HILLIARD's "Teachers Must Learn."

Harlequin Romances . . . 6 exciting novels published each month! Each month you will get to know interesting, appealing, true-to-life people . . . . You'll be swept to distant lands you've dreamed of visiting . . . . Intrigue, adventure, romance, and the destiny of many lives will thrill you through each Harlequin Romance novel.

Get all the latest books before they're sold out!

As a Harlequin subscriber you actually receive your personal copies of the latest Romances immediately after they come off the press, so you're sure of getting all 6 each month.

Cancel your subscription whenever you wish!

You don't have to buy any minimum number of books. Whenever you decide to stop your subscription just let us know and we'll cancel all further shipments.